Battle Lines

Ravenswood Crime Series 3

Tony Millington

City Stone Publishing

ISBN (paperback): 978-1-915399-32-8
ISBN (ePUB): 978-1-915399-33-5

A CIP catalogue record for this book is available from the British Library.

Tony Millington | www.facebook.com/TonyMillingtonAuthor

City Stone Publishing | www.citystonepublishing.com

June 2024

Dedicated to my family.
Ann, Richard, Jem, Dennis

"All warfare is based on deception."
"If you know the enemy and know yourself, you need not fear the
result of a hundred battles."
"Do not attack an enemy on high ground, and do not meet him
when he has the advantage of a hill."
"Siege of a city is only done as a last resort."
"Pretend inferiority and encourage his arrogance."

Sun Tzu (544 BC – 496 BC)
Author of *The Art Of War*

PROLOGUE

Trapped and struggling to break loose from the bands that tied his arms and legs, he screamed out for help.

None came.

He had been driving home in his green Saab 9-3. As the early evening dusk was taking over, he switched on his headlights, illuminating the road ahead. Suddenly, a 4x4 Toyota pulled in behind him and flashed their bright headlights, dazzling him through the rear-view mirror.

'Bloody morons.' He adjusted the mirror as the 4x4 continued to keep their headlights on full. He slowed down and pulled over in the gateway of a field so the morons could overtake. As they moved up alongside, he flipped the V's to the male passenger in the front seat. The passenger just laughed back at him as he pulled down a balaclava over his face.

The Toyota swerved and came to a stop, blocking his Saab. Three masked figures in dark clothing jumped out and approached at full pelt. One smashed the driver's window with a hammer. Frightened, he tried to shield his head from the flying shattered glass. It covered the interior of the car; fragments were nicking his skin on his face and hands. Blood started to trickle.

Another seized the door and nearly wrenched it off its hinges. A knife threatening in hand, they cut the seat belt and dragged him out of the car. Forced him to the ground. He screamed as he felt the vicious attack of kicks on every part of his body. A foot hovered over his ankle before it came down forcefully. Crying out in pain, he felt his ankle crack. More kicks followed, to his ribs, to his abdomen. Agony speared through him.

After what seemed like forever, the beating stopped. Instead, he felt their hands on his legs and arms as they bound it with tape and dragged him to the rear of his car. He saw through swollen eyes and the haze of blood coating his face the boot being opened. Hands on his arms and legs again and he was lifted, then dumped into the boot. From his dark, cramped cell, he heard someone get into the car and start the engine.

The car drove off.

Desperate, he tried to undo the ties. To no avail. His fingers were numbed and his body ached all over, every movement agony.

The car stopped. He could hear movement outside; gravel being crunched and muffled talking. Through the bulkhead of the rear seats, he heard the rear door open. A pungent smell hit his nostrils, Petrol.

HELP. GET ME OUT. He tried to shout, but it caught in his throat. Pain racked his ribs and lungs.

Smelling burning fabric, smoke started to infiltrate the boot space. Choking, he kicked out at the boot's lock.

Soon, the smoke and heat became too much.

He took in one last breath.

—

DCI Terry Watson struggled to relax in his favourite garden chair, trying to put the ongoing pain in his arm to the back of his mind. Secretly, he was relieved that it would only be another three days before he could go back to where he belonged: at work.

Since his deep arm injury because of a knife-wielding suspect he was arresting, he had been in recovery. He smiled. What an operation that had been. He was delighted, not in the least because his best friend, Keith Monteith, had been promoted to Detective Inspector. *Fully deserved,* he thought, after what Keith had been going through. He shuddered. Losing his friend had never been so close.

At any other point, if anyone had told him he had to take two months off during the summer holidays, it would have been brilliant. Spending an enjoyable couple of months with his beautiful wife Sally and their three children, Simon, Jason, and Rachael. But the damage to his right arm, a ten-inch-long gash which required thirty stitches and physiotherapy, severely impeded him.

Six-year-old Rachael was grumpy at first, not being able to have proper daddy hugs until he explained why. She had thought for two seconds and then promptly answered with a big smile, 'I will help take care of you and make your arm better by bringing in your drinks and snacks when mummy asks me to.'

Simon and Jason did their part by taking over the gardening and washing the cars. Sally joked that he did it so he could get out of his share of the housework.

This afternoon, Sally had taken the children shopping for school uniforms and equipment. She had promised to bring a Chinese take away home for tea. The credit cards would take a battering this month!

Terry wrapped his good hand around a cold, just out of the fridge, John Smith's. Beside him on the table, the latest publications by his favourite authors, Alistair Birch, and Malcolm Hollingdrake.

Switching on his portable DAB+ radio for the cricket commentary, he closed his eyes and let the dulcet tones of Jonathan Agnew and the other commentators on the Test Match Special team describe another English batting collapse against the Aussies.

As he opened his eyes, picking up Birch's book, his mobile phone's "Bat Out of Hell" ring tone came to life.

'Hello?'

Nothing.

'Hello, who is this?'

Silence.

Watson ended the call and looked at the screen. Number unknown. He frowned.

He returned back to his book and to the cricket commentary,.

"Stokes hooks a short delivery from Stark for six to bring up his fifty.

"Bat out of Hell" rang again.

Wary now, he picked up. 'Hello?'

Utter silence.

Prank calls were becoming an irritation. Watson knew several work colleagues and friends who had them. He switched the phone off determined not to give it another thought.

A shrill sound. The house phone.

Cursing, Watson stormed into the kitchen and picked up the phone extension.

'HELLO!' he shouted.

Nothing.

'WILL YOU STOP PLAYING AROUND?'

Who says I'm playing, DCI Terry Watson?

The line went dead.

Watson quickly tried 1471. No success. The caller had left no number. He cursed again as he felt a cold shiver up his spine.

Who was this? Why did they call? Was it a threat? What the hell was happening?

CHAPTER ONE

Tuesday

AFTER TWO MONTHS, IT was the first day back for both DCI Terry Watson and DI Keith Monteith. The detective team was once again complete.

Watson was early at his desk, going through the backlog of emails. The delete button took a hammering.

Smartly dressed in a tailored suit, DSI Tanya Wright came into the office and walked straight to Watson. 'Welcome back, Detective Inspector. I see you're already deep engrossed in work! We've missed you. How's the arm?'

'Still uncomfortable, but manageable. Stitches came out after about three weeks.' Watson held up his scarred arm. 'Doctors said I was lucky because it just missed an artery.'

Picking up his mug, he followed Wright out into the main office to make a fresh brew for both of them. 'I see we have a new sign,' he nodded towards the wall near the whiteboards as he handed Wright her drink.

If they stand behind you, protect them.
If they stand beside you, respect them.
If they stand against you, defeat them.

'I thought it was appropriate after what we have been through.'

'What's the latest on the Russells?' Watson asked as they made their way into Wright's office. 'I've seen all the newspaper stories online, including the "inside sources say...",' he smirked.

'Says bollocks,' Wright agreed. 'They rejected both them and their two henchmen bail because of witness intimidation and being a flight risk. Every law enforcement and government office you care to mention would like a piece of them,' she grinned.

Watson laughed. 'That'll be something! So what's the latest news?' He perched on the edge of the coffee table as Wright sat down at her desk and filled him in.

By half eight, the DSI stood in front of the troops for the morning briefing. The place had been in a raucous mood as everyone welcomed back their two friends and colleagues. Even Superintendent Matthews poked his head in on his way to his office, to everybody's shock.

Alongside Monteith and Watson were the great and good of the Ravenswood detective force: DS Karl Lorimer, DC Emma French, and DC Paul Sandall.

'Ok folks, let's make a start.' Wright brought the briefing to order. 'First, welcome back Keith and Terry.' Everyone else in the room cheered and clapped loudly. Both Watson and Monteith stood and took a bow.

'And also... once again, our congratulations with your promotion, Detective Inspector Monteith,' Wright smiled.

Another round of cheers and claps.

'Thank you, fans,' exclaimed Monteith. 'I will be available for investigating murders, stabbings, poisonings, and car crime. If anyone requires anything else, you will need to contact my agent.'

'The first thing you and Terry will do is attend the funeral of Joseph Clayton this morning. His family may be not squeaky clean, but he was a decent man and helped us, especially in the recent past. We couldn't have closed our case without him.'

A chorus of 'hear, hear' sprung up as everyone banged their desks in support.

Watson spoke. 'We know about the funeral. Billy contacted me when Joseph died. Last of the great characters.'

'Lorimer and French, you're needed up at Gorge Farm. Somebody dumped and set a car alight last night. Oh, and left behind a body in the boot for good measure.'

'Oh, nice,' Lorimer said sarcastically. 'I'd prefer full English for breakfast, but I draw the line at a crispy body. Definitely not on the menu, thank you.'

'Don't worry,' Wright responded. 'The night shift called the pathologist out and the body is now waiting for Mac to do the post-mortem. I need you to look around the place and see if there is anything that could provide us with a clue to identify the body. See if the fire left anything untouched. Maybe the VIN number is still readable.'

'Yes, ma'am,' Lorimer said.

'Sandall, I know I promised you could attend an autopsy but not this one,' said Wright. 'I plan to join Mac at the morgue for the autopsy. Curious to see how he performs his customary magic on this burnt offering.'

'Unless you like heavy metal at full blast, don't forget your ear defenders,' Watson reminded his boss.

'As long as it's not like the music you play in your car, I think you'll be safe, ma'am,' Sandall laughed.

Monteith looked at Watson. 'Did he just disrespect the great Eric Clapton?'

Watson nodded. 'And Pink Floyd.'

Monteith shook his head. 'Now that's boarding on insubordination. Repercussions are in order.' He looked sternly at Sandall.

Watson nodded and did the same. Sandall looked confused, then chuckled before bolting for the door. Everyone burst out laughing.

'You're a pair of evil buggers, you know that,' Wright chuckled. 'He's young and new here — you two are winding him up.'

'No, ma'am,' said Watson, straight-faced. 'But nobody disrespects Eric Clapton.'

—

They travelled to the crematorium in Monteith's new silver BMW 5 Series.

'When did you pick up this beauty?'

'About a week ago. The powers that be didn't take back the wages I earned from the Russells, so I thought I would spend it on a good cause. I had to get Katie a little Kia Ceed as a make-up present, so we both did well out of it. I saw your new beast in the car park this morning.'

'Oh, the Ford Focus 1.5 Titanium. The promotion has its fringe benefits, plus both of our cars were on their last cylinders, anyway. Sally also had a wage rise to cover for all the extra work she is taking on at the school helping with SEND children. Hers is the Citroen Grand C4 Picasso for her schoolwork and the kids.'

Monteith manoeuvred his car into the large crematorium car park. Not that the funeral they were here for was big. Like most crematoriums in large cities, unfortunately, it was like being on a conveyor belt. One family waiting with relatives and friends gathering to see their loved one off, another already in the crematorium, basking glory on the deceased. And a third party just concluded.

Monteith and Watson sat watching big black funeral cars lined up, waiting to take the bereaving families away and onto wakes and parties to commemorate the departed.

Joseph Clayton's battle with lung cancer hadn't been long.

The Claytons were a help and a hindrance to the local police force. Their long-standing feud with the Andersons on the Thelwell Estate kept the police and courts busy. Each family had laid claim to half the estate and God help those who ended up on the wrong turf. The response would be swift with those who encroached on the receiving end of a battering, and their cars pelted with stones.

Joseph had frequently helped the police, especially when it would be to the advantage of his family. Only recently, he had divulged information that had closed a high-profile case in Ravenswood.

Old-school Joseph had tried to instil his "manners maketh man" into his two sons, Billy and Davy. Not successfully, according to Watson and Monteith.

'Let's see if they can behave themselves,' said Watson, as they got out of the car and walked towards the entrance of the crematorium.

The turnout was impressive. Monteith and Watson took a seat in the back, away from the family and friends from the estate. Some glanced and stared, but most recognised them and ignored the two policemen. Davy and Billy both acknowledged their presence with quick nods.

Afterwards, in the crematorium garden, Billy and Davy walked over to the two detectives. 'Thank you for coming,' Billy said as he shook hands with both. Davy followed, but promptly stood away from his brother and the cops, arms folded.

Billy continued, 'We didn't see eye to eye with you most of the time, but we know our father held you in great respect. To most of the police in this city, we are just another trouble-making family.'

'Your father was one of the city's elders who sought to help when he could,' Monteith replied. 'Only recently, we discovered why.'

'Yes. You and the Russells. Dad told us about that. Not the best family to be related to.'

'Tell me about it. Listen, the book he had that contained all the information...'

Billy grinned. 'It went up in smoke with Dad, one of his last wishes. Didn't want it getting into anyone else's hands, and we didn't want it.'

'It was in the coffin?' Monteith looked stunned.

'Looks like Dad had the last laugh,' Davy shouted gleefully.

Watson put a hand on Monteith's arm, stopping him before he could say something he'd regret. Billy shot a look at his brother and gestured towards the mourners who were making their way back.

They turned and walked to the cars.

'Sorry about Davy, he can be a prat sometimes,' Billy apologised. Davy was up ahead talking to fellow mourners who undoubtedly were inquiring about the detectives' presence.

'Nothing to worry about,' Watson replied. 'What are you going to do about your dad's unofficial businesses?'

'Keep them as they are, just as long as the Andersons don't expect they can take it over now. The estate is big enough for both families. Dad and old man Anderson made certain of that. We hope to keep it that way.'

Watson stopped and looked at Billy. 'And we hope you do. The big bosses will set their targets on other people now just to warn you. The Thelwell Estate has been on their radar for a while. With the Russells out of the way and Joseph in the ground... it could be the time they step in.'

'Thanks for the warning. We will try to keep a low profile, but I can't promise anything, especially if the Andersons get ideas above their station.'

'Just leave them to us,' Watson warned.

'Thanks for coming. You can come to the party if you like.'

'Thanks for the invite, Billy, but I think we have outstayed our welcome, judging by some looks we're getting.'

Billy shook their hands again and joined his brother.

Monteith stood by Watson, watching the funeral convoy slip out of the crematorium gates. 'You believe him?'

'About them and the Anderson family? Hopefully, some of Joseph's wisdom has sunk into their heads. If not, things will get a lot rougher.'

CHAPTER TWO

DS LORIMER AND DC French made their way up the narrow lane leading to Gorge Farm. How they could get farm machinery up and down it was a miracle, Lorimer thought, as he steered the car, trying to avoid the deep potholes on either side of the road. It was just wide enough for two cars to pass without knocking their wing mirrors. High hedges overhung the lane in places, forming archways of branches.

Rounding the large barn at the end, they spotted the burnt-out car on a gravel parking area close to the barn.

Whoever had torched it had done a great job, leaving just a husk of whitened metal resting on its axles, wheel rims flush to the ground. Inside, only the seat frames and springs remained, twisted and haunting. The bonnet blown open by the force of the fire when it had reached the engine compartment. Firemen had opened the boot to allow the SOCO team to remove the body the previous night.

Having signed in with the two assigned uniformed officers looking after the area, Lorimer and French donned protective boots and gloves before approaching the car. The head of the SOCO team, Chris Stocks, came to greet them.

'Morning detectives, welcome to a different crematorium; one I hope I don't see too often.'

'Were you here when they removed the body?' French asked.

'Unfortunately, it comes with the job. We had to wait a few hours until they made the car safe and cooled it down.'

'The sick bastards,' Lorimer said with anger. 'Whatever that poor bugger did, they did not warrant this.'

'Have you found anything of use? Anything that could help us?' French asked.

Stocks shook his head. 'Not in the car. The force of the fire just about destroyed any trace evidence, but outside there is this.' Stocks led them over to a section of gravel by the end of the barn. 'Another vehicle here. I spoke to the farmer earlier, and he said that he didn't keep his vehicles on this gravel; they're all undercover in the other outbuildings. The way they have displaced the gravel, must've been a heavy vehicle. Possibly a 4x4. One of my team is trying to get a mould of a tyre print. Ruled out the farmer's Land Rover. Not a match.'

Lorimer pondered this over. 'So there could be at least two assailants, maybe three or four. One driving the getaway vehicle, and one either forcing the driver of the car to come here, or driving it here with the body already in the boot.'

An old Land Rover made its way across from the farmhouse.

'Mr Henson, the owner,' Stocks said. 'I'll continue over here then.' He walked back to the burnt-out husk.

The Land Rover pulled up next to Lorimer and French.

'Mr Henson? We're DS Karl Lorimer and DC Emma French from the Ravenswood police.' Lorimer did the introductions as they held their IDs. 'Did you see what happened with the car over there last night?'

Henson stubbed his cigarette out on the door and flicked the end out of the window, past French's ear. 'No, not really. Watching TV, heard a large bang at about eight o'clock, the other half had just started watching Eastenders. Came out and saw the car on fire. Went back in and phoned the police,' he stated matter-of-factly.

'Did you see any other vehicles?' French asked, clearly taken aback by Henson's demeanour.

'Nope, possibly red lights moving down the lane back to the main road, but that's it. Thought it was just joyriders dumping the car and driving off. Told this to the police last night.'

'I know you did. We were just checking to see if you remembered anything else, now you've slept on it. Thank you, Mr Henson.' Lorimer turned and walked back to his car. French followed him as Henson drove off.

She leant on their car's front wing. 'What did you make of him? Seemed not interested.'

'Either that or they threatened him. If something like this took place near you, wouldn't you want to know what was going on?'

'I agree,' French said. 'There was a car fire out the back of where I used to live. All the neighbours were out making sure nobody was in the car or injured, kept people away from it, especially as it set fire to another car parked next to it. That was arson, and I don't think they caught anyone.'

'Typical,' Lorimer grunted. 'There are always spates of arson, and then it dies down. Someone knows who did it but doesn't want to snitch, especially if it's gang-related.'

'And this one?' French queried.

'It isn't joyriders. That's for certain.'

They noticed a local recovery vehicle crawling its way up the lane, knocking against branches with its cab and onboard crane. The driver advanced the barn and parked up near the wreck. Lorimer called over to Chris Stocks, who confirmed they had finished and were clearing up.

'Your place or mine tonight?' French asked back in their car, driving away.

The pair had been building a relationship over the last six months, since their trip to Manchester for a murder investigation. They'd been booked into separate rooms at a hotel on Salford Quays. But after a meal, and a stroll along the quay in the cool breeze overlooked by Manchester United's Old Trafford grounds and the BBC Media Centre, they'd only used one room. So far, they'd kept it a secret from their colleagues, knowing they'd not be allowed to work to-gether once their relationship came out.

'Depends on what you're cooking,' Lorimer joked, which earned him a punch on the arm.

'You didn't complain when I made vegetable curry the other night. In fact, you had seconds, remember?'

'The dessert wasn't bad either,' Lorimer chuckled, a glint in his eye as he took the main road into the city leading back to the station. 'Still prefer a meat-based curry, though.'

'You chose to date a pescatarian,' French reminded him.

'I didn't hear you complain when we had fish and chips last night.'

She rolled her eyes. 'Pescatarian, idiot. Fish is fine, meat isn't.'

'Mac, are you here?' DSI Wright called out from outside Mac's vacant office. The gentle music of Disturbed's version of "The Sound of Silence" was playing, not Mac's usual heavy metal.

'Mac,' Wright called again.

James McIntosh stuck his head through the rubber doors from the room next door. 'Hello, Superintendent. Thought I heard someone calling my name.' Mac's head and the rest of his body came through the door, covered in scrubs and gloves. 'Just preparing the poor burnt sod from last night for his post-mortem. We rarely get the top brass down here. Welcome to my humble abode.'

'Thank you, Mac. No, you don't, and I hope not to make a habit of it. Terry and Keith are at a funeral, and Emma and Karl are out at the farm where your guest was found. I was told it was horrendous.' She walked over to him.

Mac's face lit up, his enthusiasm for his job clear. 'Well, we will go gently with the examination. You will be on the balcony overlooking; the chiefs have banned non-mortuary personnel from the floor during a post-mortem. You can ask questions through the intercom.'

'Terry told us after the body in the garage case, so I don't mind,' Wright nodded.

'I read Keith picked up his promotion. A DI now. I must congratulate him when I next see him."

The music changed from Disturbed to Metallica's "Nothing Else Matters".

'Not your normal heavy music. I was told to expect an assault of the eardrums.'

'When something like this takes place, I respect the deceased and calm the music. Being cremated in a car fire because of an accident is bad, but when the person is intentionally confined in the boot of that car before the fire, that is horrific. That level of brutality is beyond my comprehension. Burnt bodies are never easy to stomach but with a car fire, the heat is so intense, it is not surprising we sometimes don't have a body at all — just a pile of ash.' Mac sighed. 'Sorry about the rant, but this makes my blood boil. Pun intended.'

Wright nodded. 'I bet every member of the emergency services has the same thought from time to time. Don't worry, Mac. It's good to see how passionate you are about the work you do. I have already learned a lot about pathology.'

Mac laughed. 'Great to hear. Shows I'm doing something right. Listen, before I see what our guest can tell us, do you want to look at him if only from the door?'

As they made their way into the next room, the stench of burnt flesh hit Wright's nostrils at full blast, making them tingle. Her eyes watered, and her throat became painful.

Mac turned to see her coughing and covering her mouth and nose with a hanky. 'Quite overpowering, isn't it? This one spent too much time in the body bag overnight. Here, use some of this Vicks under your nose: it will help.' He removed the tub from his pocket and tossed it over.

Through the tears, Wright just made out the body, lying on its side with arms and legs curled up in foetal protection. The face contorted into a grotesque monk-like gargoyle. Waving to Mac, she signalled she was making her way up to the gallery, the pot of Vicks in her hand.

Monteith inched his car through the traffic back into the city centre. 'I've never seen a year for roadworks like it. They seem to dig everywhere at the moment, he grumbled. He glanced over to Watson, sitting in a world of his own.

'Have you heard a word I said?'

'What? Sorry, Keith. Yes, I heard you. Had some weird phone calls last week while I was away,' he added, staring out of the windscreen at the backed-up traffic ahead of them.

Monteith grinned. 'Have you been on those dating websites again? Did someone ring you and ask you on a date? I told you Sally would find out.'

'No, I haven't,' Watson snapped. 'I am serious.'

'Wow, go on, what happened?' Monteith asked as the traffic moved forward so they were the first car at the temporary traffic lights.

Watson drew a deep breath. 'Somebody rang my mobile twice last weekend. When I answered, whoever it was on the other end said nothing, so I hung up.'

'It's a call centre,' Monteith immediately said. 'They use an automated calling system known as diallers. They connect the phone call to an agent once you pick up. But if the agent is not available, it remains silent.'

'That's what I thought the first time, but it rang again five minutes later and the same thing happened. No answer, even when I asked who it was. So, I turned my mobile off.'

'Some kids playing a prank.'

'How did they get my phone number?'

Monteith shrugged before putting the car in gear as the lights changed to green. 'Random guess?'

Watson glanced at his colleague. 'So work this one out. After I switched my mobile off, whoever it was then called our home phone.'

'Seriously!'

'I shouted hello this time. Again, nothing. Then I shouted, "Will you stop playing around?"'

'Did it help?'

Watson looked straight at Monteith. 'Sort of. They answered this time.'

'And?' Monteith was growing frustrated.

'And they said, "Who says I am playing, Detective Chief Inspector Terry Watson?" Then the line went dead.'

'FUCK!' Monteith exclaimed, both at Watson's answer and in response to the driver of a crazy delivery van who drove erratically, with no care for other road users or pedestrians.

Watson explained they had left no number. 'Possibly a pay-as-you-go phone. I couldn't work out if the voice belonged to someone older or younger. It was too muffled to distinguish.'

'Do you think whoever it was altered their voice in some way?' Monteith asked.

'Using a machine or app? Don't know. Could have been.'

'You told the boss?'

'Nope, not yet. I'll do it when we get back.'

As they turned off the main road and out of the dreadful traffic, they caught the Wild West Deliveries van up ahead. He was still driving like a nutter, well above the speed limit and coming close to hitting a woman crossing the road. The driver slammed on his brakes, pulling up just short of her. Tyre smoke billowed up and brakes shrieked. The woman shook and dashed back onto the pavement, shouting at the driver.

'I feel a word in the driver's shell-like ear is in order,' Monteith said, shaking his head in disbelief. They followed the van until it parked up in front of a row of shops. Monteith pulled in behind.

They all exited their vehicles at the same time.

'Excuse me, sir, can I have a word with you?' said Monteith as he made his way towards the driver, holding his ID in his hand. Watson, likewise, showed his ID as he stepped in front of the man.

The driver was thin and wiry and looked only to be in his early twenties. 'What? I've done nothing wrong.' He looked straight at Watson. 'That bloody woman stepped out in front of me.'

'That's not what we witnessed,' replied Watson. He noticed the pungent stink of cannabis coming from the driver's mouth. 'We followed you from the city centre, and you were driving erratically, coming close to hitting several cars. Then you almost knocked over that woman back there. Can I look at your driver's licence, please?'

The van driver looked nervous. 'I have to deliver these parcels.'

'You're going nowhere near that van.' Monteith blocked his path, having seen in through the window of the van. 'Cannabis bag and smokes openly on the passenger seat. You're under arrest for drug driving.'

'My boss will kill me,' the guy yelled as Watson put the hand-cuffs on.

'You should have considered that before you started smoking that cannabis, Mr Harris.'

'And we're not taking him back to the station' Monteith said to Watson as he walked back to his car. 'I don't want my car stinking of cannabis.' He leaned in and picked up the radio. 'I'm calling for backup. Uniform can have the delights of the stink in their van.'

Ten minutes later, with the drugged-up driver, who unsurprisingly failed a roadside drugs test, safely in the back of a police van, one of the PCs nodded towards the delivery van. 'You'll not be popular. Do you know who owns Wild West Deliveries?'

'No. Who?' Monteith asked.

The policeman laughed. 'Your favourite person, James McGill.'

'Oh shit,' Watson exclaimed. 'What's the betting Matthews gets another call from McGill claiming harassment of his drivers?'

'I wouldn't put it past him.'

Watson's phone went off.

'Bloody hell, that was quick, even for McGill,' Monteith laughed. 'That van didn't have CCTV in it?'

'It's the DSI. Hello, ma'am.'

'Are you two on the way back yet?' Watson frowned. Wright's voice was not her normal chirpy-sounding one.

'Yes, we're coming back now,' he replied cautiously. 'Just caught a drug driver or we would have been back already.'

'I need you back straight away.'

Watson looked confused. 'Anything we need to know?'

'Just get back here quickly.' Wright hung up.

Monteith glanced at Watson as he pulled away from the curb. 'What's up?'

'Don't know, wasn't told but I have a feeling something's off. We've been ordered back asap.'

It wasn't long before they found out why.

CHAPTER THREE

WHEN WATSON AND MONTEITH reached the police station, they could sense a distinctly different atmosphere. Uniformed officers were gathered in groups and offices; they all avoided making eye contact with them. Just the occasional slight nod in their direction.

'Is it something we've done, gov?' Monteith whispered to Watson as they stood by for the lift.

'Don't know.'

Monteith sniffed his armpits in the lift. 'Nope, not them.'

Watson grinned.

A pale Wright intercepted them as they came out of the lift. Beside her was Lorimer. They both looked in shock, and Wright's mascara was smudged.

Had she been crying? 'What's happened?' Watson felt uneasy.

Walking into the lift, Wright said, 'Matthews wants us. He will explain.'

They both glanced at Lorimer, who shrugged and shook his head.

On entering Matthews' outer sanctum, his assistant, Beryl looked up from her desk, her eyes red and swollen.

'Sit down, please. I will check if he is ready to see you.' Her voice was weak and croaky.

She knocked on Matthews' door and opened it enough just to pop her head in. They could hear the muffled voices of Beryl and Matthews before Matthews opened the door fully, beckoning them in.

When Wright entered, Matthews asked her if she was ok, to which she nodded.

'What's this about, sir?' Watson asked worriedly. 'Are we in trouble? Is something going on we don't know about?'

Matthews was quiet and gestured for them to sit down. He poured himself a glass of water before starting. His voice was weak.

'This morning, I received a phone call from the governor of HMP Rightwell.' Matthews paused and sipped his water. 'I am sorry. They found Kenneth Crompton dead in his cell this morning.'

Watson, Monteith, and Lorimer were dumbfounded. Shock on their faces. Their former boss, DSI Kenneth Crompton, for all that had put him in jail, had been a mentor to them all.

'What? How?' blurted Watson, fists bumping on the table.

'Nooo. No, that can't be true,' exclaimed Lorimer.

'Who killed him?' asked Monteith, jumping up from his chair. 'Are you sure it's not a mistake?'

Matthews coughed and opened his mouth. Wright put her hand on his shoulder, and said, 'Detectives, please. We're sorry and this is such a tremendous shock, but please calm down. There's more.'

'There's more?' Watson looked at his bosses.

'Yes, I'm afraid so,' said Matthews. 'Kenneth Crompton took his own life. When they unlocked his cell this morning, they discovered he had slashed his wrists and bled to death. They found a razor blade on the floor by his bed.'

A stunned silence.

Matthews cleared his throat. 'I am as shocked as you are. I know the three of you have been personally selected by him, and credit to him for turning you into the fine detectives you are today. Kenneth and I often discussed your progress, and I know he would be proud of who you are today. His crime was a black page – a page we turned, but,' he paused, 'Kenneth did not deserve to die like this. He was a great detective and a good man who made a mistake and paid for it.'

Watson stared at the floor.

Monteith got up and rammed his head against the wall. 'There is no way he would have taken his own life. Someone got to him.'

'But who?' asked Lorimer. 'Who would do that?'

'Take your pick. Over six hundred criminals in that prison to start with. A copper in prison is a big prize to get.'

'I thought he was on the remand wing away from the main prison?' Watson asked.

'He was. Listen, I don't have the full facts yet, only what the governor briefly told me before he went into an emergency meeting. I have instructed him to make sure that Kenneth Crompton's body is brought to James McIntosh's morgue for the post-mortem. I'm sure they will do this in a dignified way. We will learn then what happened. Tanya, what are you working on at the moment?'

'The only major thing is the body in the burned-out car. DC Sandall and DC French can continue with the investigation today.'

'All right, I'm ordering all three of you to take the rest of the day off.'

'We can't,' Watson objected.

'That's an order. No arguments!'

Watson parked his Ford Focus on his driveway, his mind in a whirl. He'd driven on autopilot. All he needed was to be alone. That's why he hadn't fancied having a drink with his colleagues in the memory of Crompton. Too soon, and besides, he'd never seen the logic in getting drunk to honour someone's memory. He'd pay his respects differently.

His stomach grumbled, making him realise he had not eaten since breakfast. After rustling up a sandwich and coffee, Watson retired into his home office, turning on his computer. Eric Clapton's CD *Me and Mr Johnson* quickly followed. Listening to blues seemed right.

Something niggled in the back of his mind. Something didn't feel right about his former boss taking his life. Watson detested the phrase "committing suicide". It sounded like the person concerned was guilty of a crime.

Crompton had kept his own counsel throughout the interviews following his arrest for murder, not responding to anything. Why had he done that? Watson wondered.

He moved the mouse around the computer screen, opening files to select the one he wanted. Taking a bite of his sandwich and a swig of coffee, he began reading an article he had saved months ago.

DETECTIVE INVESTIGATED
New detective quizzed over aiding murderer.

Before he'd read two sentences, his mobile rang. Absently, he answered it, eyes fixed on the computer screen. Hello, DCI Watson.'

A distorted voice spoke.

'Why is the great Detective Chief Inspector Terry Watson not with his friends at the pub but shielding at home instead?'

Watson jumped up. 'WHO IS THIS?'

'Now if I told you that, where would be the fun?'

'You are sick and twisted,' Watson cried. Phone in hand, he boomed out of the office to the front window and peeked out. Was someone watching the house?

'I am upset now, DCI Watson.'

Click. The line had gone dead. The phone showed no caller information.

'BLAST!'

Who was that? He just couldn't work out who had called him. Was it the same person who disturbed him last week? Must be. Thinking quickly, he called Monteith, who sounded like he'd had already one drink too many.

'Keith, it's Terry.'

'WHOO? Oh, Terry.' Monteith slurred.

'I can't hear you.' The pub sounded loud and packed, with Keith bang in the middle of it.

'Why are you not down here?'

Watson could hear the yells from other officers urging him to join them.

'Listen, I have just had another weird phone call,' he shouted.

'What? Can't hear you. Oh, sod it.'

He heard Monteith drop his phone, and the call finished.

Who the hell was ringing? What did they want? Watson racked his brains as he went back to his home office. Four times now they had called. This was getting worrying. He knew he would have to tell the boss.

'I'd like to report my husband missing.'

Police Constable Paula Dillon looked up from her computer in the reception of the Ravenswood Police Headquarters. Picking up her notepad and pen, Dillon approached the reception desk, looking through the safety glass at the woman standing on the other side. She looked dishevelled and worn out, with dark bags under her red eyes.

'Good evening, madam. You said your husband is missing?'

The woman coughed nervously and whispered, 'Yes, yes. Who do I need to speak to?'

'If I can take some details, I can see if someone is available to talk to you.'

'Yes, please.'

Behind the woman, two men had come in and were standing close.

'Good. First, can I have your and your husband's names please?' PC Dillon asked calmly, recognising the woman's anxious state.

'Amanda Ferguson, and my husband's name is Evan Ferguson. Sorry, I haven't been to a police station before.'

'That's ok, Mrs Ferguson. Nothing to worry about. Listen, let's chat more privately,' Dillon said as she pointed towards an empty room.

Amanda Ferguson nodded and ten minutes later, they sat down in the station's comfort room, refreshments in front of them. Amanda Ferguson sat on a sofa; Dixon and Kendall, who'd joined them, were opposite her.

'Amanda, I have brought in my colleague, PC Gary Kendall,' Dixon explained. 'This is a normal process during an interview.'

The woman got up, arms wringing. 'Interview? Am I under arrest?'

'No, no, Amanda, it's so we can note down properly all the details you give us. To start searching for your husband. Please, sit down. PC Kendall will take notes.'

Wiping a stray tear from her cheek, Amanda nodded and sat down again.

'Now, shall we continue? When was the last time you saw or spoke to your husband?' Dixon asked.

'He rang me yesterday just before he finished work. We were going out to the cinema. But he never came home.'

'Yesterday?'

'Yes, why?'

Dixon glanced at Kendall. 'Why didn't you report your husband missing this morning?'

'I've been out looking for him, asking friends and colleagues, hoping he would turn up, but nothing. You *have* to believe me!' Amanda got up again, pacing the room.

'We believe you, Amanda. We are simply making certain we have the correct information. What time yesterday did he ring from work?'

'I was watching the news, so just after six o'clock.'

'And that was the last time you spoke with him?'

'Yes, I rang his mobile constantly, but it went directly into voice-mail. I called his work, and they told me he had taken off shortly after he called me.' Amanda fell silent. She sighed and said, 'That's the last thing I heard from him.'

'Thank you, Amanda. We've only got a few more questions for you now,' said Dixon. 'Where does your husband work? And do you have the make and licence number of your husband's car?'

He works at Craven Autos. He's a mechanic there. And he drives a green Saab. Don't know the make or the plate.'

'Great. One last thing. Can you write your address and contact details?' Kendall handed his notepad and pen over. While she was scribbling, he said, 'We will pass this information on to the investigating officers and they will probably come and visit you tomorrow, so if you recall anything else, anything that could help, tell them.'

They got up and showed her out to reception, where the two men who'd come in after her were being seen by another officer.

'Thank you. I'm sorry,' Amanda apologised as Kendall walked her to the station's front door. 'I just want to find Evan. I'm worried sick about him.'

'There is nothing to apologise for,' Kendall reassured her as he opened the door. 'Is there anyone to stay with you tonight?'

'My parents are on their way, thank you.'

CHAPTER FOUR

Wednesday

IT WAS A SOMBRE gathering in Wright's office the next morning. Former DSI Crompton's suicide had sent shockwaves throughout the whole police community. Many knew and had worked for Crompton; from the original four who had personally been chosen by him, only Watson and Monteith remained. Former DCs Shaun White had transferred to the Met, and Richard Walker had left the force because of mental health issues.

'Superintendent Matthews will update us on Crompton's funeral arrangements once he has spoken to Kenneth's wife and children. It's not been decided if they will give him a forces funeral, which I understand will be down to his widow. The offer is there. Mac, I believe, will be performing the post-mortem tomorrow and we will have the report shortly after.'

'Is anybody going to sit on it in?' Sandall asked.

'Not this time, Paul. We will leave Mac to do this without us watching over his shoulder and asking questions. We are also too closely involved and, as Crompton has taken his own life, we don't want the family to think our presence at the post-mortem means there's something going on.'

'What if there is?' Monteith said slowly.

'Then we will handle it as we do with all cases.' Wright reminded them all sternly.

They all glanced at each other. It was awful that he had taken his own life, but to consider someone had murdered Crompton in prison... No.

Wright walked to the information boards. 'Ok. Where are we with the body in the burnt-out car, Karl?'

Lorimer stood and crossed to the boards. 'The car found at Gorge Farm has been identified as a Saab 9-3. There wasn't much left of it following the fire apart from its shell. The individual found in the boot had already been taken to Mac's before we got there. Spoke to the SOCO, Chris Stocks this morning. He will send through the information on the footprints and tyre tracks found at the scene later today. He said that the tracks could've come from a 4x4. The farmer, Mr Henderson, owns an old Land Rover, but we have yet to match the tracks.'

'So we could be looking at an abduction gone wrong? Or someone sending a message?' Watson suggested.

'Mac's findings might shed light on your question,' Wright said. 'He established that the individual in the boot was male. Possibly late twenties, early thirties. Had received a beating before being stuck in there. Two ribs were fractured, an ankle shattered.'

'Couldn't the fire have caused that? The heat?' French pondered.

'No, Mac was positive that the injuries were caused before the cremation. The victim's footwear had melted around the ankle.'

Wright paused. 'So, we have a badly beaten male in the boot of a burnt-out car. We don't know if he was the driver, or the car was just used as a way of disposal. How many individuals could we be looking at for this?'

Lorimer stood again. 'Looking at the crime scene, three or four. One who drove the Saab to the farm, one who drove a 4x4, and maybe one or two others who could have taken part in the beating.'

Watson was writing all the updated information down on the board. It was mounting up, but they still didn't have a name for the poor unfortunate man in the boot or the reason he ended up murdered.

'Have we spoken to the owner of the farm?' Watson asked.

'As Karl said, the owner of the farm is a Mr Henson,' French responded. 'We talked to him, but his answers were evasive, as if he didn't want to get involved. Said he only saw the car after it was set alight and maybe the rear lights of something driving off.'

'A burnt-out car with a body inside in on his land and he doesn't want to help? Was he warned off? Pay him another visit. Hopefully, he will cooperate if he learns what was left in the car.' Watson frowned. 'And are we any nearer to finding out the identity of the victim?'

Sandall looked up from his computer. 'Night shift had a distressed woman reporting her husband missing. Left work Monday evening and didn't reach home. PCs Dixon and Kendall talked to her, but it looks like no one's visited her as a follow up. I don't suppose this could be our victim?'

'Let's make sure,' Watson said grimly. 'Keith and Paul, visit her and get a description of him and a photo.' He turned, 'Anything else?'

'Looks like the distraction burglars have turned up again,' Sandall ventured.

'We didn't get anywhere with that last time?'

'No, we hit a brick wall. They've either laid low or moved to another city. But now they are back and targeting pensioners. Had five reported in the last two weeks.'

'Ok, Paul — liaise with uniform and ask what we can do.'

'Ma'am, any news on what Matthews is planning with the Thelwell Estate?' Monteith asked Wright.

'He has said nothing to me. He's been so busy, I believe he's set it aside for the time being. Why?'

'With Joseph Clayton's passing, there could be a turf war building. Just thinking it might explode and we are not ready for it.'

'I will pass on your concerns to the chief when I meet him later. True, it's something we need to monitor. Ok, anything else?'

Everyone shook their heads as they turned back to their respective desks.

Watson followed Wright into her office, closing the door behind him.

'Got a minute?'

The low sun was making dappled patterns through the trees. DC French and DS Lorimer had had a couple of near misses because drivers had been blinded by the low sun. One caused Lorimer to slam on his brakes to avoid hitting a car turning out of a side road, which had not seen him coming. Horns blared from Lorimer and other road users and the air turned blue inside Lorimer's car. He still hadn't calmed down by the time they arrived at Gorge Farm.

'Some idiots shouldn't be allowed on the road,' he snapped, getting out of the car.

'The sun was right behind you,' French replied, stretching her legs. 'They could not see the line of traffic you were heading.'

'Still bloody stupid of him to pull out. That junction has always been bad; there are always accidents there, sun or no bloody sun.'

'But you didn't hit him.'

'Good job. I would have knocked his block off.'

French walked around the car and threw her arms around him. She kissed him and said, 'But you didn't, and you didn't have to. Now pull yourself together. We have an interview to take care of.'

They walked over to the rectangle of burnt offerings on the gravel where the car had stood. Scorch marks remained on the side of the barn where the heat of the flames had licked up it.

Henson's Land Rover was parked on a paved square in front of the farmhouse, along with a yellow Vauxhall Corsa. As Lorimer knocked on the wooden front door, French noticed a twitch of the curtains.

Henson, a cigarette dangling from the side of his mouth, opened the door. 'Yes, what do you want?'

'Mr Henson, I'm DS Lorimer, and this is DC Fre...'

Henson cut him short. 'I know who you are. What do you want?'

Lorimer and French stared at the farmer.

'Mr Henson, can we come in? We have a few more questions to ask,' French said calmy.

'No, I told you all I saw the other day.' Henson took one last drag of the cigarette and stubbed what was remaining out on the wall by the door, allowing it to fall on the doorstep alongside others.

Lorimer took a stride forward. 'Mr Henson, were you threatened by whoever dumped the body in the car?'

Henson's eyes twitched, his fists clenched. 'I'm not saying any-thing else.'

'Mr Henson, if they threatened you, share it with us so we can help you. They are murderers. The sooner we get these thugs off the street the better.'

'No, I'm done with this,' he said resolutely, slamming the door shut.

They heard the bolts and locks being put back into place.

French looked at the window and saw the curtains twitch again. A woman's face appeared. They could hear Henson say something, and immediately, the curtains were closed.

'At least we're now sure he knows something,' she said as they walked back to the car.

'Yes, but the problem is getting him to tell us.'

———

'So, what's this about you dissing Terry's music?' Monteith asked Sandall as they were approaching Amanda Ferguson's house.

'What?'

'I overheard you didn't like the rock music he was playing in the car. Wasn't it Pink Floyd you complained about?'

Sandall laughed. 'I was joking. Terry claimed he didn't under-stand all of today's technology. That poor girl Alison Grant was wearing a Fitbit when she was taken, so I was explaining to him what it did. He had taken the mickey out of me before, so I figured it was payback time haha. Him listening to CDs and vinyl instead of downloading and streaming music.'

Monteith chuckled. 'Terry told me. He also said you did some particularly valuable work on that case. If it wasn't for you, we might not have caught that bastard. You connecting the dots with the fencing, that's what broke the case.'

Sandall flushed. 'Thank you. I was only doing my job.'

Monteith turned into Amanda Ferguson's street and parked the car. 'We all are doing our jobs, but it's that one fragment of information or clue we find that makes all the difference. You found it this time. Next time, it could be Karl or Emma. What you did hasn't gone unnoticed, so continue the way you're going, and you'll make a good detective. One warning though,' Monteith added, straight-faced. 'Never diss the music.'

They burst out laughing as they exited the car.

'Compose yourself,' Monteith warned as they walked up the driveway.

The door of the Ferguson house was open, and a young man was leaving, kissing Amanda on the cheek as he went.

'Amanda Ferguson?' Monteith introduced both himself and Sandall as they displayed their IDs. 'I wonder if we could have a moment of your time.'

The man turned around and looked at Amanda. 'Do you need me to stick around?'

'No, it's all right, Joey. I'll be fine.' With that, he was off.

'Who's that?' Monteith asked.

'My brother Joey. He's been with me for most of the morning, trying to keep me sane. Are you here about my husband? Have you found him?'

'Yes, Mrs Ferguson we are, and no, we haven't yet. May we come in?'

'Sure.' She led them through into the living room.

'Don't you want your brother with you while we are here?' Monteith asked.

'No, it's fine, detectives. He needs to get to work. Please sit down.'

Monteith sat down on an armchair and looked around the room. 'Now Mrs Ferguson...'

'Amanda. Mrs Ferguson sounds so formal.'

Monteith looked at Sandall, who was standing by the front window. 'Ok, Amanda, you came into the station last night to report your husband missing.'

She blushed. 'Yes, can you apologise to that nice woman PC? I might have been a bit snappy.'

'No worries, Amanda. We'll now go over what you told, so we're sure we have all the details,' Monteith continued while he went through Amanda's statement with her.

Having concluded that, he asked, 'You said your husband works at Craven Autos. That's on the Barton Industrial Estate, right?'

'Yes, normally he takes about twenty minutes to drive home, depending on the traffic, of course.'

'I assume your husband hasn't come back or been in contact since last night?'

'No detective. I would have said so,' she said primly.

'Is there anything else you can remember? Did you argue?'

'Detective,' Amanda's voice was cold. 'I appreciate that one of your leads of inquiry is always the family, but trust me, we have a solid relationship and no, we did not have any argument.'

Monteith nodded. 'Amanda, do you have a photograph of your husband? It would help us. Also, we can use it in appeals for his whereabouts in the local media.'

'Yes, take this one,' she said, getting out of her chair and over to a cabinet. Picking it up, she handed it over to Monteith.

'Thank you. One more question, I'm sorry to ask, but does your husband have any mental issues? Could he be suicidal?'

Her eyes sparked. She bit, 'No detective. Evan is fine. Life and soul of the party. Not a man who commits suicide.'

After Monteith handed Amanda his card, he and Sandall took their leave.

As they got into the car, Monteith asked, 'What do you think of her?'

'She's either in denial, or she is one cold-hearted bitch and doesn't care.'

Monteith chuckled. 'And that Joey isn't her brother, that's for sure.'

CHAPTER FIVE

THE BATTLE LINES ON the Thelwell Estate had been drawn between two rival families, the Claytons and the Russells, who could trace their family tree back to when Ravenswood had only been a small dot on the map. Their dividing lines were pretty clear; the status quo suited the police, but it also meant they were unable to catch criminals. What happened on the estate, stayed on the estate. Activities were transferred rapidly once the police were on track.

That didn't stop the police from carrying out raids, and occasionally arrest criminals, but usually, they were outrun by them. Tip-offs from individuals who knew people and the local lookouts helped.

Now the Russell brothers were out of the picture, the Anderson family under father Edward "Woody" Anderson had decided to step in and fill the vacuum. After the funeral, Woody had approached Davy and Billy Clayton to set up a meeting.

'Cordial meeting,' Davy raged. 'Dad is only just cold in his urn, and they want to meet. Nothing the Andersons do is cordial.'

'I know,' Billy admitted, 'but let's just see what they want before we decide how to play this little game.'

'I don't like it! Dad passes away and they suddenly want to talk.' Davy shook his head. 'The last time Dad and old man Anderson tried this, three ended up in the hospital and another five in court, including us. Our families are like oil and water; they don't mix. They can stay in their little part of the estate, as it has been since we were knee-high to a grasshopper. I want it to stay that way.'

The pub door opened and in strode Woody Anderson with his three sons, Andrew, Freddie, and Luke. Walking towards the Clayton brothers in the back, he nodded to Freddie and Luke, who took up a position at the bar. The atmosphere was thick with tension. The regulars were at pains to give the two families a wide berth by sitting and standing at the other end of the pub.

Billy stood up, kicking Davy under the table for him to follow. Cursing, Davy got also up.

'Mr Anderson.' Billy shook Woody's hand. Davy kept his hands down by his side, flexed, in case anything happened. He glanced around the room, making a mental note of who was where.

'Billy, Davy, thank you for seeing me,' Woody said and took a seat. They all followed.

'First, once again, my condolences. Your father was a re-spectable man.'

'Thank you, Mr Anderson. We appreciate your kind words,' Billy replied. Davy snorted with disgust.

'You wanted to talk?'

'Yes, Billy, I won't beat about the bush. Join us. Create a joint... enterprise, if you will, between our families.'

'What?' Billy exclaimed.

'Fuck off,' said Davy, enraged. He got up, fists balled.

All three Anderson sons got up too, ready to fight. The barman moved the glasses on the bar out of the way.

Woody held his hand up. 'Calm down, boys. We all know Joseph was the brains behind your business, somebody the estate looked up to and took notice of. Sadly with his passing, that leaves you two out of your depth. I merely offer you a chance to combine forces and split the spoils. You can still be in control of your half of the estate.' He smiled. 'Under my leadership.'

That was too much for Davy. Before Billy could react, Davy'd launched himself over the table at Woody. 'You fucking bastard,' he shouted out as he knocked everything off the table. Andrew responded quickly with a punch to Davy's face and a left swing at his head. The two other brothers restrained Davy, pressing his face on the table. Billy tried to intervene, but got hit several times.

'You bastard Anderson,' Davy continued to shout. 'You're a dead man.'

Woody Anderson knelt face to face with Davy. 'Looks like you're in no position to make threats.' He stood up, brushing dust from his trousers. Scowling at Billy, who was standing doubled up in pain, 'That was stupid. Next time, we won't be so gentle.'

He signalled, and his sons backed away from Billy and Davy towards the door. Davy grabbed a glass, but the barman and Billy got hold of him before he threw it.

'I suggest you leave by the back door, Billy,' the barman said after the Andersons had left.

Billy stood up straight. 'We don't use the back door anywhere.'

The drive back home was in stony silence. Once the front door had slammed shut behind them, Billy exclaimed, 'What the fuck were you playing at?'

Davey pointed a finger at his brother. 'What the fuck do you mean? I was playing at something? You were about to jump into bed with Woody! They needed showing we need no help.' He bristled, fists balled.

Billy stepped back. 'Calm down, brother. Fighting them in public is not the way to get the better of them. That's what they wanted us to do, and you fell straight into it. You know the Andersons were nothing under the Russells. Now they've gone and our dad has passed. Woody smells blood. He wants in.'

Red-faced, Davy shook his head. 'The nerve of that man. They want us off the estate now dad's gone. First they share, then they take over fully and we're out. We need to fight fire with fire to save face. We are the Claytons and we should be the ones to lay down the rules.'

'And we will, my dear brother, just be patient.'

'PATIENT! The sooner we are rid of the Andersons, the better.'

'I agree.' Billy placed his hands on Davy's shoulders. 'I don't trust a word that comes out of their mouths. I never have, but Dad seemed to have a way of dealing with them. Didn't you learn anything from him?'

'He's not here now, is he?' Tears were streaming down Davy's face.

'I know he's not,' Billy said soothingly. 'So, it's down to us to carry on with the business. Listen, take your hatred and frustration out on the punching bag in the garden. I have a few phone calls to make.'

As Davy trudged out through the kitchen to the back garden, mumbling incoherently, Billy sat down with the phone and his thoughts. Dealing with the Andersons was one thing: dealing with Davy's ever-increasing anger another. Their dad could handle Davy. Whatever he said, Davy did without question. But now, it was down to him to keep a lid on Davy's anger. He could hear Davy's grunts as he started thumping the hell out of the punching bag. *Good, just what he needs.*

Sending Davy to anger management classes had proved a waste of time. He'd punched the counsellor. And he seemed on first-name terms with the magistrates at the court... A question of being there too often. The bank had a direct debit set up with the courts to pay for all the fines Davy had accumulated.

Billy dialled a number.

The owner answered on the fourth ring.

'Mr Anderson, it's Billy Clayton. Can we meet again, just the two of us?'

Thursday

James McIntosh knew this would be one of the hardest autopsies he had ever done.

Former DSI Kenneth Crompton's body had arrived from HMP Rightwell in a private ambulance during the previous afternoon. Mac and his assistant took their time in taking Crompton out of the body bag and onto one of the examining tables. They removed all his blood-stained clothing, bagging and tagging it, before sliding Crompton into one of the cold chambers. The deep cuts on his wrists spoke for themselves.

The rain and dark clouds outside matched the mood Mac was in, so he slipped Kiss' *Destroyer* CD in the car's CD player and struggled to rock into a better frame of mind before he entered the mortuary. It worked until he saw Watson's car in the car park.

Mac parked up and dashed through the rain, knocking on the passenger window to get Watson's attention before climbing in.

'What the hell are you doing here, Terry? I thought we agreed that nobody from the office would show up for this.'

'I... I was on my way in and just thought...'

Mac lowered his voice, seeing Watson struggling. 'What did you think, Terry?'

'I needed to see him. Say goodbye.'

Mac sighed. 'This is neither the time nor the place. His funeral is. You don't want to see your old boss and friend in the state he's in.'

'But...'

'No buts. I'm not letting you in. For your sanity, for one. And DSI Wright asked me not to.'

Watson shot a look at Mac.

Mac put his hands up in mock surrender. 'Listen, it didn't matter what she said to you two, she knew either you or Keith would come. I'm only acting on her instructions.'

Watson bowed his head. 'I know, Mac, you're right. It's just, you know.'

Mac nodded. 'No problems, Terry. I'll bring the findings as soon as I've finished the post-mortem. Kenneth is getting priority, I have made sure of that. The other stuff can wait.' He opened the door and got out.

'Thanks, Mac,' said Watson, closing the door and driving away.

The rain had become heavier, the clouds darker. Neither man seemed to notice.

Billy Clayton wished he had a jacket in the back of his car. It hadn't been raining when he left, but now the windscreen wipers were on full, as were the headlights. Summer was ending in a big way.

He knew that he and his brother had big boots to fill after their dad's passing. That is why he had set up another meeting with the Andersons, without Davy this time. He'd probably be still in bed, Billy mused, after another pub crawl last night. His brother's drinking and fury had increased lately. He wouldn't be surprised if Davy was using drugs. His behaviour was so irate.

Billy parked up facing the entrance at The Dragon's Den car park, one of the many pubs that hadn't survived rebranding their old-fashioned pubs into a sports bar or upmarket food pub. He killed the lights and waited, keeping the engine on and the wipers going. The rain had eased, but it still was coming down relentlessly.

His fingers drummed on the steering wheel. *Where were they?* After twenty minutes, he decided to leave. It was then that he saw two cars turning into the car park. Anderson had come with backup. 'What was I thinking?' Billy muttered, frustrated.

The cars swung around and pulled in next to Billy, one on each side, so close that Billy couldn't open the door. Andrew and Luke glowered at him. Billy's nerves were on edge.

Woody Anderson emerged from the other car along with Freddie and stepped around their car to Billy's. Freddie opened the rear door for his father and then got into the front himself. Billy looked in the rear-view mirror at Woody.

'I thought we agreed it would be just us two?'

'One thing you need to learn in business, legal or illegal, don't come to the table without a backup plan,' Woody answered.

'And these three are your backup plan?'

'I go nowhere without them. Right, Freddie?'

'Yes, Dad.'

Woody continued. 'Anyway, I already knew you wouldn't be bringing any backup. Luke and Freddie saw Davy smashed out of his brains and taking drugs in town last night. I take it he's still nursing his hangover?'

Billy grew more anxious. So he had been right about Davy taking drugs. Were they following him and his brother?

Woody was growing impatient. 'So, what do you want? You called me.' He clicked his knuckles.

Billy swallowed hard. *Sorry, Dad, but I have to do this.* 'You mentioned you wanted us to come and work for you. A joint enterprise, I think you called it. I accept your offer, deal, or whatever you want to call it.'

'And what about Davy? Aren't you going to ask him?'

'I can handle Davy.'

Woody thought about it for about ten seconds. 'Sorry, that deal is off the table.'

'What!'

'Let's call this in industry terms... a hostile takeover.'

Freddie's fist smacked into Billy's nose. Blood spurted down his front and all over the driver's side window. Pain seared through him. Tears welled up and streamed, mingling with the flow of blood running from the now broken nose. Through blurry eyes, he noticed Andrew and Luke laughing their heads off in the other car.

'You had your chance before your dickhead of a brother fucked it all up,' Woody reminded him. 'Now we are taking over the full estate. I issue you with a winding-up order. Leave the estate while you have a chance.'

With that, Freddie and Woody got out and back into their car. Both cars disappeared out of the car park and out into the increasing morning rush-hour traffic.

Sitting there battered and bruised, Billy slowly regained his senses. 'He wants to take over... Two can play *that* game.'

CHAPTER SIX

'Boss, the report from SOCO Chris Stocks has come in,' Sandall called as he returned from the printer. Watson joined him by the whiteboards.

'Right, what's first?' Watson asked, marker pen in hand.

Sandall scanned the report. 'They have identified the car as a Saab 9-3, colour green. I thought a fire like that would have removed all the paint?'

'It's fascinating what the SOCO bods can turn up with when most people expect there is nothing to detect,' Watson replied, writing the information on the board. 'Anything else?'

'They pulled tyre marks from three different vehicles close to the scene. One came from a tyre used on Land Rover Discovery.'

Lorimer looked up. 'Mr Henson, the owner of the farm, has one of them.' He got up and walked to the board.

'So, his tracks will be all over the site,' Sandall commented.

'Yes, they will, but he said they don't use that part of the farm. They are all parked in the barns or up by the farmhouse. He also claimed he only saw the fire from the farmhouse and didn't go anywhere near thinking it was only joyriders.'

Watson turned to face him. 'If those tyre marks were fresh, he could have been closer than he said.'

French, who had been also listening, joined in. 'When we visited him last, he was definitely on edge. We asked if he had been threatened, and he clammed up and shut the door on us.'

'What are we thinking? He returns to the farm either before or after they set the car on fire. He pulls over to see what was going on and was threatened?' asked Watson.

'Sounds like a plausible theory,' Lorimer agreed.

'The other tyre tracks,' Sandall read again from the report. 'One is a bog-standard tyre track which could have been from the Saab, but they are not certain. The last one is from a 4x4, perhaps something like a Toyota Land Cruiser but other 4x4 are available. Hang on a minute,' Sandall sat back at his desk and logged back into his computer.

'That firms up another part of the theory. The buggers that did this disappeared in a 4x4 as we thought. Check,' said Lorimer, making a tick sign in the air.

'Thought she mentioned it,' Sandall slapped the desk.

'Who?' asked Lorimer.

'Amanda Ferguson.'

Watson and Lorimer looked confused.

'Amanda Ferguson, the woman who reported her husband, Evan Ferguson, missing. I went with Keith yesterday to her house to do a follow-up interview. She said Evan drives a green Saab.'

Watson asked Sandall, 'Did Mac find any personal effects that survived the fire?'

'Erm... I don't know, but I can check with him.'

'I thought you went to the post-mortem?' French asked.

'No, the DSI went. But I haven't heard her mention anything about personal effects. I wish I could have done it. That's two I have missed out on.'

'You will get your chance if you get promoted to sergeant,' Watson reminded him. 'Have you seen one now you're a sergeant, Karl?'

'No way,' Lorimer shook his head said. 'You are not catching me anywhere near one of those.'

'Now who's the wimp?' French joined in.

Lorimer looked at French with his arms out wide. 'Hey, I thought you would be on my side.'

'Not on this one. You're on your own.'

'Cheers.'

'What's this? An argument?' Monteith strolled back into the office, with Wright following behind. They had been in Superintendent Matthews' office.

'NO!!'

'YES!!'

Everyone shouted simultaneously.

'Stop it, children,' said Monteith mockingly. 'What's new, Terry?'

'Hang on, just let me finish this. Lorimer and French, bring in farmer Henson for a formal interview.'

Both nodded and walked out of the office.

Watson turned to Wright and Monteith and told them the latest information. 'And that, ma'am, is why I want Keith to take Sandall and go to Mac, see if he has any personal stuff from the burned-out Saab. If so, Keith, could you please visit Amanda Ferguson with a family liaison officer in case she recognises anything?'

Monteith nodded. 'I'll get right onto it.'

'Wait, you two. I want to speak to you in my office. Now, please,' said Wright.

She strode towards her office and sat down behind her desk, which was covered with files and paperwork. She waited for both to sit down.

'Terry, while you were parked up over at Mac's this morning, and yes, Mac rang me after you left, Matthews called Keith and me to his office.'

Watson opened his mouth, but she held up her hand to stop him.

'He had had a phone call from one James McGill.'

'We've not been anywhere near him or the Barton Industrial Estate. What's that idiot said now?' Watson exclaimed.

'Calm down, Terry. Keith explained your last run-in, so I know what type of jerk he is. This time it was about that van driver you collared for drug driving. McGill owns Wild West Deliveries.'

'We heard that from one of the uniforms who brought the driver in. What's he accusing us of this time? Let me guess - planting cannabis on his driver?'

Wright nodded. 'Spot on.'

Watson grumbled. 'I hope Matthews told him he was mistaken?'

'He was ringing him as we were leaving his office. Listen, you were entirely justified arresting that driver. Don't let McGill get under your skin. If you two keep doing your job properly, you won't get any complaints from me.'

Monteith and Watson thanked Wright and got up.

'Terry, do you have a minute?'

Monteith closed the door behind him as Watson sat down again.

'Want to explain about this morning?'

He shrugged. 'Nothing to tell.'

'Really? Mac finds you sitting in your car in the pouring rain in the hospital car park and you say there is nothing to tell?'

Watson frowned but said nothing. His fingers were picking imaginary fluff of his trousers as he stared out of the window.

Wright kept silent.

'I can't believe he's gone,' he finally spoke. 'And I refuse to believe he took his own life.'

Wright came around and perched herself on the front of her desk. 'I cannot imagine what you're going through, but sitting outside the morgue will not help. Think of the man you served with instead. All the good days you had, the ones you and Keith talked about the other day. Those are the memories you need to hold on to.'

———

Billy Clayton staggered in through his front door. Making his way into the kitchen through the front room, he searched in the medicine cabinet for painkillers. Filling up a glass with water, he downed the tablets before running warm water in the sink and stripping off his blood-soaked top and trousers and shoving them into the washing machine. He stood there in just his boxers in front of the kitchen window, wiping the congealed blood from his face and hands. He winced when he touched his nose.

He went upstairs to put on some clean clothes. It was almost lunchtime and Davy still hadn't appeared. It must be one hell of a hangover, Billy thought grimly.

Had he done the right thing meeting the Andersons? His nose said it all. NO. But at least now he knew. Things wouldn't go back to the way they were when their father was alive. That had died with him. He wished he could talk to his father, to discuss what to do.

Davy's door opened. He took one look at Billy's face and exploded.

Monteith and Sandall arrived at Amanda Ferguson's address at the same time as the family liaison officer, PC Sharon Walsh.

'Hello detectives,' Sharon said as she locked her car. 'Grizzly business, this one.'

'You can say that again,' Monteith nodded.

'We are hoping she might recognise these,' Monteith took out two evidence bags out of his jacket pocket. 'This wedding ring and the charred chain and what's left of the wallet in the other one are the only things we have to identify the body. Mac is still waiting for DNA confirmation.'

The three of them made their way up the driveway. Amanda Ferguson opened the front door so fast it smacked against the peach-coloured wall behind, the handle leaving a dent in it.

'Have you found him?' she said, agitated.

Monteith spoke softly. 'Amanda, can we come in? We have an update.'

Amanda's face crumpled.

The man behind her said, 'You go in love.'

He held out his hand to Monteith. 'Hello, I'm Nigel Highfield, Amanda's father. We came down from Lincoln yesterday.'

Monteith shook his hand and introduced his colleagues as they entered the house.

Amanda was sitting on the couch, hands clasped together. An elderly woman got up.

'Hello detectives, I'm Emily, Amanda's mother.' She shook hands with them and they sat down.

This was the part of their job they hated. Telling someone their loved one had been found dead. You never got used to it, especially with children and young adults. Those with all their lives to live before them before it abruptly ended. They had all seen officers crumble with the burden of doing it. Even seasoned officers with years of experience.

Monteith took a deep breath. 'Amanda, we have discovered a car that we believe resembles Evan's car.'

Amanda blurted out, 'Where is he? Is he all right? Can I see him?' She gripped her mother's hand tightly.

Monteith reached into his jacket pocket and pulled out the two evidence bags.

'Amanda, can you have a look at these, please? Do you recognise them?' He passed them across to her. Amanda's hands were shaking. She ran her fingers over the bag with the ring and chain.

'Ca... can I open it?' she whispered.

Monteith nodded.

She let the chain and ring fall from the bag onto her lap. With trembling fingers, she picked up the wedding ring. 'Does this mean.. is Evan...?' She looked imploringly at Monteith.

He hesitated, then nodded. 'It seems so, I'm afraid.'

A piercing cry erupted from Amanda as she fell into the arms of her mother. The chain dropped to the floor. Nigel Highfield reached down and picked it up, mouthing to Monteith to follow him into the kitchen. He closed the door behind them.

'I'm sorry but I don't wish my daughter to hear this, inspector. I saw the state the chain and ring were in, and with my thirty years of being a fireman, now retired, I recognise fire damage.'

They could hear Amanda sobbing in the living room.

Monteith leant back against the kitchen sink. 'Evan's car was discovered on farmland. By the time emergency crews arrived, the car was well alight.'

'Arson?'

'Yes, I'm sorry, Mr Highfield.'

The man stared at him. 'And Evan? Where was he?'

Monteith paused just too long.

'Detective, I have seen things as a fireman I wish I hadn't. Things that always remain with me. I ask again, where was Evan?'

'Tied up in the boot. He had been beaten before being put in there.'

The colour drained fast from Highfield's face. Monteith quickly pulled a chair out from under the kitchen table so the man could sit down, and handed him a glass of water. The kitchen door opened and Sandall walked in. He looked questioningly at Monteith who nodded.

After a sip of water, Highfield looked straight at Monteith. 'You get the bastards that did this to my son-in-law? Promise me.'

Monteith leaned forward. 'Promise. We'll have our best detectives on this.'

'Good. I'd ask you to leave now. I'll break the news about Evan to Amanda when she's ready.'

Monteith agreed. 'You're right. PC Walsh will remain with you as your family liaison officer. Any information we come up with, or if Amanda can recall anything that would be useful, PC Walsh will pass it on.'

As they reached the front door, Walsh handed Sandall the two evidence bags, much to the protestations of Amanda.

'How long are you and your wife staying?' Sandall asked as High-field opened the door.

'We'll probably have to nip to Lincoln on Saturday for clothes and check the house, but we will be back in the evening.'

'Is there anybody who can stay with Amanda while you are away? I'm just thinking in case PC Walsh is not around. Brothers or sisters?'

'No, no family. Our son Darren lives in Chicago. Moved out there for work six years ago.'

Sandall thanked him and joined Monteith.

'Told you Joey wasn't her brother.'

CHAPTER SEVEN

Watson and Monteith settled themselves with beer in Watson's home office. Sally knew that what Terry called "brainstorming" was more for the two men to offload what they encountered at work, seeing the dark side of life. She let the men to themselves, and kept the children away, glad that the two good friends had each other. Crompton's suicide had hit them hard.

She could tell how drunk they were getting by the heated discussion and arguments. She smiled. Best therapy, she thought.

'What are you saying? Crompton deliberately set out to murder Colin Littlewood?' Monteith struggled to comprehend what Watson had suggested. 'I can go along with he shot Littlewood because of what he was threatening to do with Smith and McNulty, but murder! Why?'

'Something he said has been niggling me since that day.' Watson took a glug of John Smith's before continuing. 'As he handed over his gun, he said something about that woman, the woman who ran the pub where Freeman was killed. What's her name?'

Monteith racked his brains. 'Erm. Liz. Elizabeth Preston.'

'That's her. He mentioned her. I didn't know why. And he never revealed the reason for killing Littlewood. All he said was no comment during the interrogations.'

'Because Freeman was her brother?'

'Yes. And I suspect Crompton had a thing for Elizabeth Preston.'

'What?' Monteith exclaimed, trying but failing to get up from his chair. 'That's bollocks. He was a proud family man. I fight anyone who dares to say differently.'

'Not now, you drunken prat.' Watson waved a hand of disgust at his friend. 'Before he got together and married his wife, Edith. Probably around the time he was a PC or newbie detective.'

'He and Preston were an item?' Confusion was etched on Monteith's face.

'It's looking that way.' Watson passed across an article he had pulled off his computer. 'Read this. This was a newspaper article from when Ronald Freeman was convicted for the murder of a local shopkeeper, Fred Mason.'

DETECTIVE INVESTIGATED
New detective quizzed over aiding murderer

'See? It says that the Independent Police Conduct Authority had interviewed Crompton because he knew the Freeman family. It gets worse. Crompton admits to having been in a relationship with Ronald's sister, Elizabeth Freeman.' Watson explained. 'It further says the relationship fizzled out, but the allegation was that Crompton had prior knowledge of the robbery and did nothing to prevent it. An allegation Crompton refuted strenuously.'

Monteith blew his cheeks out after reading. 'Lack of evidence is why the IPCA cleared Crompton. I'm sure he didn't know, he would have reported it! But now I understand why you thought he was keeping something back when Freeman was killed.'

'Yep, and I was right. Do you remember him disappearing every so often, saying he had a meeting or an appointment?'

'I think so.'

'On one of those occasions, I spotted his car outside the Dragon's Den, the pub Elizabeth Freeman Preston ran.'

'You think he was still seeing her?'

Watson shook his head. 'No, but I bet he told Elizabeth he would get the man who murdered her brother. And the standoff on the multi-storey was the perfect place. Armed police all around, Littlewood waving a gun around and threatening to kill McNulty and Smith.'

'If that's the case, where did he get the gun? He didn't have it when we went to Claythorn prison before the standoff. We had to hand over everything we had on us to security. He didn't have it then.'

'He had. The only place he could hide it then was in your car.'

'WHAT?'

'Oh yes,' Watson nodded. 'He put it out of sight either in the footwell or stuffed it down the side of the back seat when we went into the prison.'

'The bastard. What if he had left it there? Rebecca and Pixie sit in the back.' Monteith was furious.

'Keith, I get you man, but calm down. He didn't in the end.'

'I'd twist his head off if he was still alive.' Monteith put his head in his hands. 'Oh God. Sorry, Terry, I didn't mean that.'

The door to the office opened, and Sally stood there.

'As always, your timing is impeccable,' Terry nodded towards Keith. 'We need a break.'

'Katie called, asking whether you will grace her and the kids with your presence tonight.'

'Oh bugger, I forgot the time. Can you call me a taxi?'

'YOU'RE A TAXI,' Sally and Terry said in unison.

'Ha bloody ha.'

Ten minutes later, a taxi containing a rather drunk Monteith pulled away.

'Will he be all right?' Sally asked.

'Yes, he'll be fine,' Watson replied, his arm around his wife.

'And you?' Sally asked as she shut the front door behind them.

Watson sighed. 'I don't know.' He burst into tears.

Sally wrapped her arms around him.

———

Davy Clayton stood out of the way of street lighting at the entrance of an alley, looking at Anderson's home. A blanket of cloud covered the moon to add to the darkness.

Anger raged throughout his body. Billy had told him what went on at the meeting. A meeting he should have been at. The argument between them had lasted most of the day before he stormed out of the house.

He still hadn't forgiven Billy for not telling him and going on his own. His brother had done well, only coming back with just a broken nose. Other people who had gone up against the Andersons had suffered worse.

Their father had drummed into both of them, 'Don't start the fight, but if someone starts on you, make sure you are on the winning side.' The Andersons had started this fight, so God help them.

He would love to go over there right now and fight them. Four against one? No problem. But this time, Billy was right. Going head-to-head would be wrong. They needed to come up with a plan to get rid of them permanently. Davy slipped away into the darkness.

Friday

Watson picked up Monteith early the next morning. He always moderated his drinks so he wouldn't get hangovers. Unlike Keith, he smiled wryly.

When he knocked on the door, a bleary-eyed Katie opened it.

'Take him to work, please,' came the exasperated plea. 'He's been nothing but trouble since he got back.'

Monteith was in the kitchen knocking back a large glass of water along with painkillers.

'How's the headache?' Watson asked as he slapped his friend on the back.

'Piss off and stop shouting.'

Watson laughing. 'I'm not shouting. It's your hangover.' He turned to Katie. 'What happened when he got back?'

Katie folded her arms in front of her chest. 'What didn't happen? First, he could not get his key to the front door, so he rang the bell, waking the children. Next, he fell up the stairs. Then Rebecca and Pixie heard their father vomiting in the bathroom. And finally, after spending ten minutes undressing and getting into bed, he thought we would have sex until I put pay to that with a swift knee to his privates.'

Watson winced. 'Ouch nasty, a hangover, and ball ache.'

'Just take him. I have two exhausted and grumpy kids to get ready for school.' She disappeared up the stairs. 'Rebecca, are you washed yet?'

Monteith crawled into the passenger seat wearing dark glasses. Watson was tempted to set his music on full blast on the way into the headquarters, but looking at his colleague in such a delicate state, he took mercy on him by playing Pink Floyd's "The Wall" softly. "Comfortably Numb" came on next. He smiled. How appropriate.

Once inside, Monteith told Sandall to do the briefing, handing him his notes.

'Evan left Craven Autos on the Barton Industrial Estate at six o'clock. Should have taken around twenty to twenty-five minutes to get home. We know that somewhere between Craven Autos and his home, Evan was attacked and transported to Gorge Farm.'

'Gorge Farm is nowhere near either place. It's in the opposite direction.' Watson was studying the map of the city and its surrounding area on the wall, inserting pins in the three areas of interest.

'I think it would be a good idea for you and me, Keith, to talk to Evan's colleagues,' Watson said. 'Unless you have any objection, ma'am. You know that James McGill also has businesses there?'

Wright grimaced. 'I know. I expect and trust that you two act in a manner fitting of two of our best detectives.' She paused. 'And let me remind you both that I don't want to hear Matthews going at you again for provoking McGill.'

—

Lorimer and French had put Geoffrey Henson and his solicitor, Franklin Trainor in an interview room twenty minutes ago to allow them time to talk. They had been unsuccessful in bringing him in the day before, when Henson's wife claimed he'd been at the wholesalers in Norwich. To make sure he complied this time, they'd taken two uniformed police officers with them to pick him up.

Henson was complaining about why he was brought in, even after having been informed about the body in the boot of the burned-out car.

'I have explained to my client the serious nature of not cooperating with you,' Franklin Trainor stated as soon as Lorimer and French entered the room. 'And that you could charge him with impeding an investigation if he didn't. Hence, Mr Henson would like some guarantees on his and his wife's safety.'

'Thank you, Mr Trainor,' Lorimer said as they sat down at the table, Lorimer opposite Henson. 'I will take what you have said regarding assurances on board, but it is not up to us to give them. We understand that Mr Henson is worried about his safety, but it will depend on what he tells us to see what is possible. Especially considering the last time we spoke. Mr Henson was less than forthcoming.'

Trainor turned and whispered something into Henson's ear. Henson shook his head, but then sighed and nodded.

'My client will cooperate.'

French turned on the recording tapes and all of them said their names for the record.

'Mr Henson,' Lorimer started. 'Thank you for coming in and helping us with our inquiries.'

'You gave me no choice,' Henson grumbled.

'Geoffrey,' Trainor admonished his client.

Lorimer looked straight at Henson. 'On Monday evening of this week, you reported to the police that a car was on fire on your property, Gorge Farm. Is that correct?'

Henson nodded.

'For the benefit of the tape, Mr Henson, can you reply yes or no to my last question?'

Henson looked at Lorimer. 'Yes.'

'Thank you. Now please, Mr Henson. Can you tell us in your own words what happened on Monday evening?'

Henson looked again at his solicitor, who nodded for him to continue.

He nervously shuffled in his chair. 'I was coming back to my farm and had turned into the lane when I saw a ball of flame coming from close to one of my barns. I thought someone had set fire to it. So, I sped up and got to the barn as quickly as I could.'

'What did you see when you got there?' Lorimer asked.

'I saw it was a car and not my barn, thank God. The car was well alight when I got there.'

'Was the car yours?'

'No. I don't keep any vehicles out near that barn; they're all kept undercover. Except for mine and the wife's, they're always parked by the farmhouse.'

French took notes. Lorimer continued. 'Thank you. What happened next?'

Henson glanced again at his solicitor. His left hand went through his hair as he continued. 'I went to get out of my Land Rover but was stopped. Someone came out of the gloom and struck the Land Rover. Scared the living daylights out of me, it did.' Henson's voice faltered.

'Struck it with what?' Lorimer asked.

'A baseball bat. He hit the wing of the Land Rover and shut the door on me.'

'Did he say anything?'

'Yes, he muttered something through his balaclava.'

'Mr Henson, the more information you can provide us, the better chance we have of catching these murderers.'

Henson looked like he was having an internal battle. His head bowed; his hands clasped together. 'He said to drive away if I knew what was good for me,' he almost whispered. 'Or I would end up like the man in the car's boot.' His voice broke.

Trainor suggested a break. Lorimer nodded, and French stated for the tape that the interview was suspended.

Wright was waiting outside in the corridor as Lorimer and French emerged.

'Now we know why he was reluctant to help,' French said as she leant against the wall. 'We are dealing with vicious individuals. Can we give him and his wife some security? They might come back and carry out their threat.'

Wright nodded. 'I'll arrange uniforms for detached duty. That's as much as we can offer for now because of budgets. When are you going back in?'

'In a bit. Give Henson time to pull himself together,' Lorimer said. 'It took a lot to tell us that. Hopefully, he can give us a description of the perpetrators.'

Ten minutes later, they re-started the interview.

'Mr Henson,' Lorimer said. 'When the man threatened you, did you see anyone else?'

Henson frowned and took his time. He looked like he was adding up numbers in his head. 'I think there were three, no, four. One who shouted at me, two who stood back from the burning car, and I think there was one getting into another car. I think it was a large 4x4.'

Lorimer glanced at French and nodded. Their hunch about the events proved right.

'Mr Henson, were all of them wearing balaclavas, or could you see their faces?'

After another hesitation, 'I think they all were. I couldn't see their faces. They were dressed in black. With the shadows from the barn and the fire, it was difficult to see.'

'That's fine. Can you describe the vehicle the man got into?'

'I don't know,' Henson hesitated. 'I think it was dark blue or purple, can't be sure.' He winced.

'Detectives,' Franklin Trainor said. 'As you can see, Mr Henson is having trouble. I think we need to stop this interview. He has answered all your questions.'

Lorimer agreed. French switched off the tape.

'Thank you for your help, Mr Henson. In case we have any follow-up questions, we'd like to contact you.'

Henson nodded. 'No problem.'

'Ok, let's check if the safety measures have been arranged.'

CHAPTER EIGHT

WATSON WAITED ON THE road leading to the Barton Industrial Estate for the large, refrigerated lorry to finish backing into a loading bay of a chiller company. The driver had been taking his time moving backward and forwards because of the number of cars and other lorries parked on the road.

'How's your head?' Watson asked Monteith, who was still wearing his dark glasses.

Sipping on water, Monteith shrugged. 'Better. Now it's a dull ache. I wish he would hurry and park.'

'Do you remember anything from last night?'

'Nope, but Katie made sure I knew this morning.'

'I bet she did,' Watson laughed. 'The state you were in.'

The lorry completed a twenty-five-point turn, enabling the disgruntled drivers to finally move off. Watson followed two cars and a delivery van through the gates of the industrial estate. Craven Autos was easy to spot, halfway down the first block of units on the right-hand side. Its signage was large and bright. Watson parked up in the only available space in front of the unit.

Monteith took off his glasses as he got out of the car and walked towards the custom car repair shop. 'Wow. I'm in love.'

Inside, three cars were being worked on, all in various states of being customised. One was up on a ramp; its exhaust being removed. Another had its bonnet open with two men raising the engine out with chains and pulleys.

'Can I help you?'

A young man wearing a Craven Autos polo shirt came out of a rear office.

'Detective Chief Inspector Terry Watson and this is Detective Inspector Keith Monteith.' They showed the man their IDs. 'We are looking for the owner.'

'You've found him, Ryan Craven.' The man held out his hand.

'Nice setup you have here,' Monteith said, looking around. 'What services do you offer?'

'All modifications and tuning. You name it, we do it. Lowering suspension and springs, fitting customised exhausts, remapping and re-tuning engines. In terms of the bodywork, adding fabricated body kits, and you can have your windows tinted.'

'What are they doing to that Dodge in the corner?' Watson was pointing to two men with what looked like a large roll of sticky-back plastic.

'It's a unique concept. Vehicle wrapping.'

Both Watson and Monteith looked bemused at Ryan Craven.

'It's a different approach to changing the colour of your car, and a lot cheaper than having a full body respray. You can have whatever design you want. And it won't damage the original paintwork if you want to sell the car. You can remove it quick and easy.'

'Don't get any ideas, Keith, you have only just got your car,' Watson reminded his friend, who was drooling over the cars.

'Anyway, you're not here to talk about cars. Evan Ferguson, I guess?' Craven led them into his office. He cleared two chairs of magazines so Watson and Monteith could sit down.

'Detectives, I rang Amanda last night to see how she was, so I know what happened to Evan,' Craven said. 'Spoke to her father, who told me the horrible details.'

Monteith pulled out his notes. 'Mrs Ferguson told us that on the evening he went missing, she phoned here to see if he had left. That would be around seven?'

'Yes, that's right.'

'But you shut at six?'

Yes, we do. I had remained to finish some paperwork and place orders for the equipment we needed. Seven would be right; I was just about to leave when she rang. Asked if Evan was still here. I told her he'd left bang on six.'

'How was he when he left?' Watson asked.

'He was ok, looking forward to going to the cinema; they were seeing *Bohemian Rhapsody,* the film everybody's raving about.'

'How long had Evan been working here?' Monteith continued.

'Ever since we set up, that's seven years. We were an MOT, tyre, and repair garage then. But with the big companies undercutting our prices, and overheads with this place, we couldn't compete. So, about a year ago, we changed tack and went into custom cars.'

'And you have never had any problems with him?'

'Nope, nothing.'

Watson leaned forward. 'Has a customer threatened you or any of your employees?'

Craven looked puzzled. 'What? You think it's someone with a grudge against me or the business?'

'We don't know, but it's something we need to consider.'

'We have had a few disgruntled customers who thought we hadn't done an acceptable job on their cherished possession, but enough to kill Evan? No way.'

They got up. 'Thanks for your time, Mr Craven.'

'Let me walk you out.'

A young mechanic was heading out of the unit. 'Just going on my lunch, Ryan.'

'Ok Joey. Don't take too long. We need to complete that Porsche by Friday afternoon.'

'Back in thirty.'

Craven turned to Watson and Monteith. 'Excellent worker, Joey. Started with us when we switched to custom cars. A whizz with suspensions and wheels. Taught me a thing or two.'

Monteith nudged Watson. As they reached Watson's car, Joey was speeding off in his car.

'What's up?' Watson asked, pressing his key fob.

'That Joey. Thought I recognised him. He was just leaving Amanda Ferguson when I went with Paul to see her first time around.'

'So he's a workmate.'

Monteith scoffed. 'He's more than that. He kissed Amanda on the cheek when leaving, and when we asked her who he was, she replied he was her brother.'

'He can be both Evan's colleague and Amanda's brother.'

'When Paul asked Amanda's father the last time we were there, he said she had a brother who lived in America. And his name is not Joey.'

'Aha, now I see what you're getting at. She's playing away. Wonder how long that's been going on. Do we follow him?'

'No, let's get back. We know where to find him. Anyway, it's lunchtime and I'm starving. Fancy a large fry up, Terry?'

No response. Monteith looked at Watson. 'Terry?'

Watson was facing the row of buildings across from Craven Autos. James McGill stood in the entrance to his unit, watching. Watson made a beeline straight for him. Monteith hurried behind. 'Wait.'

Watson approached McGill.

'I could have you for harassment,' McGill snickered.

'We've been nowhere near you or your business,' Watson responded.

'Didn't you know I back Craven Autos? My name may not be over the garage, but it's my money.'

Monteith grabbed Watson's arm. 'Terry, don't. Just walk away.'

'Listen to your friend and walk away,' McGill grinned. 'Oh, and thanks for arresting Harris. Didn't know about his drug taking. You did me a favour there.'

Watson's face flushed with anger. 'Didn't stop you from saying to Matthews that we planted it,' he hissed.

'Terry, leave it. Let's go and grab lunch.'

They were lucky to find a table inside the teapot cafe behind the city's market, a hive of activity around lunchtime. A group of four market traders had just got up from their table when Watson and Monteith finished ordering at the counter.

'Here's to your cholesterol. How you can eat one of their big breakfasts is mindboggling.' Watson swirled his mug of tea in the air.

'I'm at the peak of fitness, I have you know. Doc checked me over when I was off.'

'Good to hear. Don't want you dropping dead on me anytime soon.'

Monteith looked up as the cafe's door opened. 'Talk of being at death's door. Look at Billy Clayton.'

Billy and Davy Clayton walked in, deep in conversation. Billy's nose was taped up, and his eyes were black and blue. Watson waved for them to come over to their table, the only two seats still available.

'You look like you have been in the ring with Anthony Joshua,' Monteith said.

'One round with Freddie Anderson, the prat,' Davy grumbled.

'The Andersons? What have you been up to?'

'We've done nothing. They have declared all-out war on us,' Billy spatted, nostrils flaring.

'What? I thought your families were ok.' Watson was concerned.

'Nope,' Billy said. 'Shortly after the funeral, Woody called and asked if we could meet up on neutral ground. When we got there, he said the two families should go into partnership, and work together.'

As he was talking, a waiter brought them three bacon and sausage baps and Monteith's huge fry-up.

Davy stared at the plate. 'You're not going to eat all that?'

Monteith grinned as he sunk his knife and fork into a sausage.

'Rather you than me!' Davy said, shaking his head.

Billy took a bite of his bap and continued, 'Anyway, Davy here put pay to that original meeting when he launched himself over the table at old man Anderson.'

'Not the best cause of action.'

'And I would have got to him if it wasn't for his sons,' Davy butted in. 'He deserved a broken nose for even thinking we would join them.'

'So how did you get your bust nose, Billy?' Monteith asked in between mouthfuls of fried bread, egg, bacon, sausage, tomato, hash browns, and baked beans.

'Woody agreed to meet me again yesterday, just the two of us. He brought his sons. Davy was incapacitated,say, shall we say, so it was just me.'

Davy grunted in disgust.

'I said we would accept his offer, but he said the deal off the table. Then Freddie did this,' Billy pointed to his nose. 'He now has declared all-out war on us, wants us off the estate.'

Watson wiped his mouth. 'I warned you not to go up against Anderson.'

'They started it,' Davy muttered.

'Yes, so you've said, and where did it get you? Billy with a broken nose and you with your ego damaged. They have confirmed that they want you gone, so stop aggravating them and leave the Andersons to us. If they carry out anything against you, let us know and we will deal with it.'

Davy jumped up. 'When? You have said to us before that the police will clean out the estate of crap families and,' he jabbed his finger at Watson, 'YOU HAVE DONE NOTHING.'

'Calm down, Davy,' Billy said.

'No, I won't. It's about time someone told them. Old man Anderson still struts about like he owns the place. And he does. What is done about it? Nothing at all.'

Watson moved swiftly. Before anyone realised what was happening, he'd grabbed Davy and face-planted him on the table, forcing his arm behind his back. He lifted Davy, who was screaming in agony, off the table and frog-marched him out of the cafe. Billy chased after them.

Monteith calmly stuffed a last fork full in his mouth, before grabbing his ID and getting up. Showing it to the startled customers, he said, 'Police business. Nothing to be alarmed over.'

Outside, Watson shoved Davy up against a wall and grabbed him by the lapels. 'Don't you ever, *ever* do that again to either of us. If you do, you will find yourself in a cell.' He shook his head. 'Look at you. What's the matter with you? If your dad could see you now.'

'Dad, dad, that's all I hear. Dad did this, dad did that. He is not here now, is he? It's just me and Billy. The Andersons have said we are nobody. *No one* calls the Claytons a nobody and gets away with it.' Davy wrestled free of Watson's grasp and raced off.

'You had better run after him,' Monteith told Billy. 'God knows what he will do.'

Billy nodded. 'Wish me luck.'

Monteith turned to Watson, who was panting. 'Are you all right?'

'Just about. Let's get back to the station.'

James McIntosh normally didn't visit the police headquarters. All his reports were emailed over or someone picked them up at the morgue. Today was special. Today, he would personally deliver Kenneth Crompton's post-mortem report out of respect for him and his former colleagues. He had called ahead to DSI Wright to say that he was on his way. She had instructed him to bring it directly to her office.

As McIntosh walked into the main office, the chatter stopped. Lorimer, French, and Sandall looked in his direction. They knew why he was there.

'Hello, lads, Emma.'

'Hi Mac,' Lorimer returned the greeting. 'Terry and Keith aren't here, but they are on their way in. The bosses are in there,' he added, nodding to Wright's office.

'Mac,' Wright called, beckoning him into her office where Matthews was already seated.

Mac took a deep breath as he walked into Wright's office.

'As you can see, my verdict is DSI Kenneth Crompton took his own life by cutting both his wrists, causing severe blood loss. He used the razor blade found in his cell. I discovered his skin and fingerprints on the razor blade. No one else's. The toxicology report is clear; he was not under the influence of any substance.'

Matthews briefly scanned the report before handing it over to Wright.

She took some time to read it, after which she lifted her eyes to Mac. 'Thanks, Mac. I'll share this with the team.'

In the briefing room, the tension was palpable when Wright shared the details of the report with the detectives.

'But do we know why?' Lorimer asked.

'We might have a theory on that.' Everyone turned to see Monteith and Watson standing by the door. Watson scraped his throat before explaining their theory of what had happened around the murders of Ronald Freeman and Colin Littlewood.

'That's pure speculation,' Matthews commented.

'Yes, at the moment it is, sir. But can you think of anything else that would make a respected DSI kill someone like Littlewood, keep his own counsel during interviews, then take his own life?'

Matthews frowned. 'Hmm, you have a point. Has Elizabeth Preston been informed of his suicide yet? She may have something to tell us.'

'Do we know if she visited Crompton in Rightwell?' Monteith asked. 'In fact, have we checked to see the visitor's log? Could someone have told him something which led him to commit suicide?'

'I will talk with the governor at Rightwell and ask for the visitor's log to be sent over. Right, I have places to be,' Matthews said. 'Thank you, Mac, for your due diligence and thoroughness. The force and the family thank you for it. I will pass on your conclusions to Crompton's family so they can start arranging his funeral.'

'Will it be a full police funeral?' Lorimer asked as Matthews was leaving.

'No. From the conversation I had with his widow, she said they would like just a small family one. I will represent the force. Anyone of the detectives who want to attend, be there informally, not in uniform. I'm sure she'll not mind that.'

'Thanks, sir. I know I speak for all of us when I say we'd like to be there if we can,' Watson stated.

Matthews smiled and nodded. 'I expected you would.'

CHAPTER NINE

JAMES MCGILL STRODE ACROSS the industrial estate as if he owned the place. With two companies of his own and a couple of others he had put money in, he was close to doing so.

Ryan Craven was shutting up for the night as he spotted the figure of McGill heading his way. 'What the fuck does he want now?' he mumbled.

'I saw you had Pinky and Perky visiting earlier,' McGill sneered.

'Who?'

'The police. Who do you think I meant?'

Craven unlocked his car. 'Oh, DCI Watson and DI Monteith. They were asking about Evan.'

'You didn't tell them anything?'

'Of course, I didn't. I'm not stupid.' Craven got into his car, but before he could start it, McGill grabbed the driver's door and yanked it open, leaning down on eye level.

'I wasn't finished. What did you tell them?'

Craven looked nervous. 'Nothing. They asked me how long he had been working for me, and what was he like. I played their questions with a straight bat.'

'Good. Keep it that way. Remember, I rescued your business. I can take that away again,' McGill threatened.

Craven drove away with McGill's threat ringing in his ears. He cursed for being manipulated by McGill's terms of support a year ago when he was fighting to save his business. Now McGill had control of the garage. Being bankrolled by such a man turned his stomach. But what could he do now? He *had* to make a decision. If he didn't get out now, he could end up like Evan. He shivered with fear.

—

Amanda Ferguson sat in the garden with her dad. She felt numb. The last days had been an emotional rollercoaster. She still had difficulty believing Evan was dead. Gruesomely murdered. Her husband, her soul mate. Gone.

The family liaison officer, Sharon Walsh, had been helpful. Not pushing for details, just being there. Amanda found it easier to talk to Sharon than her parents, especially when she needed to vent her fury and anger. But Sharon had gone now for the day. Emily, Amanda's mother, was busy in the kitchen and her father took the opportunity to talk to his daughter.

'How are you?'

Amanda smiled weakly. 'Shattered. The last few days are catching up. I haven't slept all week. Just catnapped.'

'I know. We could hear you downstairs early this morning.'

They could hear the phone going off in the house; Emily appeared at the back door with the phone in her hand.

'Amanda, it's the police, a DSI Wright for you.'

Nigel got up. 'Do you want me to take it, love?'

Amanda nodded. 'Thanks, Dad.'

He walked towards his wife and took the phone into the living room. Entering, he took the phone from his wife and walked through into the living room. Amanda could not hear what was being said, but when her dad had finished, he came out again. 'We have a busy day Monday.'

Saturday

The morning was a damp one after overnight downpours. Puddles littered the uneven concrete and tarmac as James McGill parked his Mercedes in his personal space outside his firm, Wild West Deliveries.

The first drivers were already loading their vans with boxes and parcels. The seven tonners lined up waiting for the forklift loaders to put shrink-wrapped pallets full of goods on board.

McGill dropped his briefcase, suit jacket, and a newspaper in his office before searching out his right-hand man, Travis Whiteman. It was Whiteman who delivered McGill's orders when he wasn't around. A brute of a man with a shaved head and both arms full of tattoos.

'Everything ok this morning?' McGill asked.

'Yes, boss. No trouble,' Whiteman confirmed before shouting across the unit, 'Adams, get that van out of here. You're late.'

'On my way,' a young driver replied as he got in his van and shot out of the unit, almost knocking over some of the other drivers.

McGill shook his head. 'Who has the special packages today?'

'Adams, that's why I said he was late. And Greatbatch.'

'He had better get there on time.'

'He will. Adams is a surprisingly good driver considering his age. One of the best we have.' Whiteman studied the paperwork on his clipboard as another van pulled out of its assigned space. The driver leaned out of the window to talk to Whiteman.

'Morning, Greatbatch.'

'Morning. Everything checked, boss, special packages on board.'

'Good. You know where to take them. Make certain they're your first drop.'

'Will do.' With that, Greatbatch was on his way.

An hour later, with eight other vans and four seven-tonners out of the door, the two of them were sorting out paperwork in McGill's office.

'No problems with Harris?' McGill asked.

'No, he's gone, the stupid bugger. I told him about drugs being banned when he joined last month. Smoking that stuff, especially while he was out driving, was idiotic. And being caught by those detectives was... well, poetic justice.'

McGill sighed. 'He isn't getting help from me when he goes to court. Also, those two detectives are becoming very troublesome. First humiliating me in front of the estate when that nutter crashed that car the other month, then arresting Harris. Yesterday, they were over at Craven's.'

'Did he say anything?'

'No, he wouldn't dare. He knows who pulls the strings and who can cut them at any time. I made sure to let him know his obligations.'

'He'd better not. We've put too much into building this up to see it go because of loose tongues,' Whiteman said. 'Evan Ferguson learned that.'

McGill's jaws tightened. 'That bastard almost cost us. Anyway, whose idea was it to dump the car in a farmyard and set it alight?'

'That was Greatbatch. He was driving Ferguson's car. Thought it was safe to stick it behind the barn. Didn't count for the owner to come back, did he?'

McGill stared at Whiteman. 'You made sure he will keep his mouth shut?'

'Who, the farmer? Oh yes, he was sufficiently warned,' Whiteman grinned.

'And he didn't recognise anyone?' McGill pressed.

'No, we kept our faces covered, and I was the only one who spoke.'

'Good, otherwise we might have to pay him another visit.' McGill opened up the laptop and browsed online. He frowned. 'WHAT? Have you seen this?' he shouted.

Travis looked over his shoulder at the article on the local newspaper's website.

Police have issued an appeal for information regarding a car fire on local farmland. They were called to Gorge Farm in the early hours of Tuesday morning to discover a car well alight.

DSI Tanya Wright said, 'We are convinced that this was more than a joyriding stunt. We would like to get in touch with the driver of a dark blue

4x4 seen in the farm's vicinity late on Monday
evening. They may have noticed something.'

'Calm down, boss,' Travis said. 'They didn't mention Ferguson's body in the car. Maybe there wasn't anything left of him.'

McGill was furious. 'Calm down, my arse. I bet it was that bloody farmer who blabbered.' He banged his fist on the desk.

Travis shook his head. 'You don't know that. There are a few houses around the farm, and we passed a couple of cars on the way back. One of them could have talked to the police. Anyway, Craven has dealt with the 4x4. They won't find it.'

'At least that's one piece of good news. Have Adams and Great-batch reported in?'

'They just texted to say that all the packages were delivered safely. The customers are thrilled,' Travis smiled.

Paul Sandall sat in the living room of his one-bedroom flat, enjoying his lunch. He felt lucky to have landed the position of detective constable in Ravenswood. Four months in and he was still relishing every minute.

Only weeks after passing his detective exam, he'd spotted the job vacancies at the Ravenswood CID and he immediately applied. To his amazement, he had been one of the lucky eight who came through the first round of over a hundred applications, so he was told. He and Emma French had made it. He smiled. Lucky indeed.

They'd been dropped in the middle of it when one of their own had gone missing. An opportunity for him and Emma to show their capability. What did they call it? A rapid learning curve. You couldn't get any faster. Collecting all the information that was coming in from the search teams all around the city and disseminating it, had been bordering on mindboggling.

Then he had been paired up with his DCI, Terry Watson. Terrified at first, he pondered, Watson quickly had taken him under his wing. He had been surprised that he'd been allowed to come up with suggestions and follow them up. They got to save a woman and arrest their killer, who'd by then been responsible for ten murders.

He smiled. That had felt good. As had the praise everyone had given him. A huge lift, knowing that all his hard work and efforts were getting noticed. Even by the Chief Superintendent.

Emma looked like she had fallen on her feet as well. He suspected that there was more going on between her and Lorimer but he didn't want to pry. She clearly kept it to herself, and he couldn't blame her. Good for her, Paul thought, as he got ready to go into town. His parents were constantly asking them why he wasn't getting married with children, like his elder brother and sister. Paul didn't want to get married early. Career first. At twenty-eight, he was in no rush.

He slung on his jacket, picked up his car keys and wallet, and headed towards the lift. As he waited, he heard a large groan and a few swear words coming from the stairs. Turning to see who it was, he spotted a large box on legs taking the stairs one by one. As it neared the top, the box dropped and the swear words became louder. Paul snatched the box before it struck the floor.

'Thank you.' A woman dressed in jeans and a see-through t-shirt gasped as she finished climbing, stretching her back.

Sandall grinned. 'Why didn't you use the lift?'

'It looks like it's out of order. I waited ten minutes before I came up. Two flights of stairs kill carrying boxes,' she gasped, still out of air.

'That's the third time in as many months these lifts have not been working.' Sandall didn't recall seeing the woman before. 'Are you moving in here? I didn't know an apartment had come available.'

'Yep, I'm moving into number eighteen.' A smile lit up her face.

'Welcome. I'm across the way in number nineteen. Do you want help with this box?'

'Please, my arms feel like they will drop off.' The woman fumbled around for her flat keys. 'I'm Caroline, by the way.'

'Paul. Nice to meet you.' He lifted one box and carried it to her flat door.

She opened the door and he went through to the kitchen, putting it on the worktop. The flat had the same layout as his, but the opposite way around.

'Are there any more boxes you need to bring up? I can help if you like?' Paul suggested.

'That's ok, thanks for the offer. My sister is helping me move in; she should be up shortly. And my dad is coming with the van later.'

There was a loud banging on the door. 'Caroline, where the hell are you? This box is bloody heavy. What have you got in it? And that bloody lift is out of order.'

'That'll be my sister,' Caroline said as she walked to the door to open it to another large box on legs.

Paul shot forward and took the box from the sister, adding it to the one in the kitchen.

'Where the hell were you? I thought you were coming back down?' Caroline's sister asked. She noticed Paul and her eyes darted over his body.

'Paul, this is my sister, Jordan. Jordan, this is my new neighbour, Paul.'

'Well, hello. Does this hunk come with the flat? I think I will come over more often, sis. I might even move in with you.'

Paul chuckled. He'd better make his excuses. 'Ladies, nice to meet you. I'll leave you to get settled in.'

When he stepped outside, Jordan slapped his backside, a smirk on her face. Paul grinned as he shut the door behind him. He could hear the giggles of both sisters as he walked off. *Things were looking up.* Then he remembered the lift was out of order.

'Bugger.'

CHAPTER TEN

FREDDIE ANDERSON QUICKLY PUSHED the doors wide open as an old, battered Vauxhall Cavalier swung in front of them, closing them after the car had entered the garage.

The Andersons were at one of their three garages dotted around the Thelwell Estate. The wooden-fronted storage unit was situated in a nondescript back alley. No one would suspect what took place inside.

Behind the dull frontage was a hive of activity. If Craven Autos dealt with the top-of-the-range cars, this was the autos equivalent to Poundland. Stolen cars from all around Ravenswood ended up in this chop shop.

The Andersons had a small group of smart car thieves. They identified which cars were easy to break into and made to disappear. As soon as they stole one, they'd drive it to one of the three garages, all hiding in plain sight, to be cut and shut. How many of them were on the road was anyone's guess.

Billy and Davy were aware of the chop shops; they knew about most of Woody Anderson's businesses. Now they needed to use that knowledge to fight him.

Behind this garage was a heap of rubbish. Plastics, cardboard, old tyres, bits of metal in containers along with oil, petrol, and gas canisters. A pyromaniac's birthday present. Billy and Davy would love to light up the lot, with the Andersons and their team inside, but not today. Not with kids playing on the road, and the local football club Thelwell Warriors playing on one of the pitches at the back of the place.

Soon they would take action, but not now.

———

Monteith's house was full of laughter, and that was just the adults. The final BBQ of the summer was in full swing, and the Monteiths and Watsons were celebrating.

Terry and Keith held forth over the meat cooking, operating two gas-fuelled BBQs. With nine mouths to feed, they needed it. Every space in the kitchen was filled with plates of food and drink. The fridge was bulging, and they required extra iceboxes for the beer. This summer was going out with a bang.

'It's fascinating that Keith thinks he's the greatest cook ever when the BBQ is out,' Katie joked.

Sally smiled. They were watching their husbands through the kitchen window, wine glasses in their hands. 'I know. Terry is the same. True, he does his fair share in the kitchen when he can, but the BBQ seems to bring out the Hairy Bikers in both of them.'

'Without the hair, thank God,' Katie replied.

Sally giggled, nearly spitting out her wine. 'Definitely without the hair. Ugg, I hate hairy men.'

Remember last November when they grew moustaches for Movember?'

'I know. It was like kissing a wire brush. I have had to warn Terry from doing that again or he will get nothing during that month, never mind a kiss.'

'Give me a clean-shaven face any day of the week,' Katie responded.

'Agreed,' Sally said.

They clinked glasses.

With a glint in her eye, Katie said. 'I wouldn't kick Jason Momoa out of bed, though.'

'Katie!' Sally laughed. 'Add Tom Hardy and I might join you.'

'You might join her with what?' Terry asked as he stepped through the back door carrying a plate of freshly cooked burgers, followed by Keith with a plate of sausages, and five hungry kids.

Sally and Katie burst out laughing. 'You wouldn't understand, dear,' Sally said as she placed a kiss on Terry's cheek.

Terry winked as he put the plate down on the table.

'Right kids, plates at the ready. Who's for food?' Katie asked as all five kids clamoured around the table.

'Time for a refill, eh, Keith?' Watson handed out another cold beer to Monteith. 'At least you don't have far to stagger tonight.'

The men stepped outside, letting the kids have the first load of food.

'More than my life's worth if I get slaughtered today, if you know what I mean,' Monteith replied.

Watson's phone rang in his pocket. He looked at the call identifier, "Unknown," and decided to ignore it. The call stopped.

'Another one of those calls?' Monteith noticed the confused look on his friend's face.

'Looks like it. Not had one since we were told about Crompton, and you were in the pub.'

'Yer, sorry about that. I dropped my phone in my beer.'

Watson's phone went off again. "Unknown." Standing up, he warned Monteith he would take this one.

'Hello.'

'Not answering before was not very helpful, was it?' The voice on the other end was distorted as before.

Watson put the phone on speaker. He kept his cool. 'You have me at a disadvantage. You seem to know me, but I have no idea who you are.'

'And that's the way it will stay for now. By the way, your BBQ smells wonderful. It's making me feel hungry.'

Alarmed, Watson and Monteith looked at each other. 'WHAT?'

'I'll be back in touch soon. Bye.' The call ended.

Monteith set off for the back door before Watson grabbed his arm.

'I don't want to alarm the kids, Katie, and Sally.'

'But he's nearby. We can catch him,' Monteith shouted.

Katie and Sally turned to the men. 'Everything all right?' Katie called out.

Monteith stared at Watson before relenting. 'Yes, darling. Have the kids left us any food?'

'Yes, come and get it.'

Watson pointed out, 'If we went charging through the house, by the time we reached the front door, whoever this is will have long gone. And we would have upset kids and angry wives. We need to get a handle on who this is. I don't have the foggiest because of the distorted voice. I have told the boss about these calls. Once I tell her about this last one, we need to get the tech bods on it. It's not a crank caller.'

Monteith nodded. 'About time we turned the tables on this nutter. First, let's eat - I need something to soak up this beer.'

———

Sandall came out of the last shop on his list; he needed a drink and a bite to eat before heading home. Hopefully bumping back into those lovely sisters Jordan and Caroline, that would round off the day perfectly. He smiled, picturing the three of them. Now *that* would be something.

Entering Starbucks, he placed his order and stood by at the end of the counter for his drink and food. Glancing out of the main window, he startled. I know them, he thought. But from what? The couple went into the shop opposite. Looping his shopping bags over his wrists and with his drink and food on a try, Sandall made his way to a vacated table by the window.

After about ten minutes, the couple came out of the shop, giving Sandall a good view of them. *Interesting*, he thought as he watched them walk down the street, glancing into other shop windows, unaware that someone had spotted them.

Sandall made a quick note on a paper napkin. With a smile, he pocketed it in his wallet before attacking the large piece of cake in front of him.

———

The night sky above the Thelwell Estate was glowing with bright reds and oranges. The glow could be seen all around. In amongst the colour, dark smoke billowed with the wind. The stench of tyre rubber, cardboard, and plastics was unbearable. The fire service had issued orders for the houses around to keep their windows and doors shut, not easy on this warm night.

Two fire engines and four police cars blocked the road. This was dangerous with the amount of different combustible ingredients that had caught fire or were close to the outbreak. People from neighbouring houses were moved out because of gas cylinders at the back of the workplace where the fire had started. Other cylinders were understood to be inside, along with petrol and oil.

Everybody knew who the owners were. But this was the Thelwell Estate. Loose tongues were punished.

Monday

Leads on the Evan Ferguson murder were non-existent even after the press appeal over the weekend. The talk all over the station was regarding the fire over on the Thelwell Estate and unease was permeating through the station.

Superintendent Matthews was sitting in on this morning's briefing because of the lack of leads. Matthews and Wright had agreed for the local newspaper to put it out on their website. But only with the limited details Geoffrey Henson had provided, and no mention of a body.

'The Hensons have a uniformed presence in the area, and they call in every couple of hours to the farmhouse,' Matthews confirmed. 'They didn't want to go into witness protection, but have agreed to let us know their whereabouts if they leave the farmhouse. Can't stop the production of the local farmers. So next, have we been to Evan Ferguson's workplace?'

'We went there Friday. Craven Autos,' Watson replied. 'The owner, Ryan Craven said that Evan had been working there since the place opened seven years ago. He had been a solid worker, no problems at all. Popular with the customers and knew his way around an engine.'

'Don't know if it's anything,' Monteith continued, 'but one of the other workers, Joey, was around at the grieving widow's when Paul and I went to speak to her.'

'And I spotted them in town together on Saturday afternoon,' Sandall added.

'Were they now?' Watson replied, adding the new information on the board. 'Fed up with husband, starts an affair with a colleague, has husband bumped off.'

'A bit far-fetched,' French said sceptically.

'Why? It's more common than you realise,' Watson explained. 'The classic Black Widows are the best known.'

'I'm sorry?' French said.

'They're named after the spider. When a female black widow spider finds a mate, she eats him after having sex.'

French rolled her eyes. Lorimer winked at her. Thank god no one saw that, she thought.

Wright took over. 'Okay, leaving that aside, the local radio station is putting out the appeal at midday with a contact number for Crimestoppers and the 101 number. We will see if anybody knows something. I told Amanda Ferguson's father, and he agreed to come down to the station for an update and to ask her more questions.

Keith and Paul, will you look after her? She knows you and should be relaxed.'

Matthews added, 'If they are ok, we may look to the possibility of a police appeal on the local television, with it being such a hideous crime. Can you ask her if she would be up for that?'

Watson nodded. 'Yes, Paul, make sure you ask that.'

'Yes, boss. Do we mention anything about Joey?' Sandall asked.

'Why not? We don't have any idea yet of why Evan was murdered so we need her to give us some background on the marriage. Was it in trouble? Even if it's only to rule her out,' Watson confirmed.

As the briefing broke up, Watson's office phone started to ring. 'DCI Watson.'

'Sir, it's the front desk. I have Billy Clayton here.'

'Billy Clayton? Did he say what it was about?' Watson was curious.

'Only says he needs to talk to you urgently.'

'I'll be down shortly, thanks.'

Monteith stood by the office door as Watson put the phone down. 'Trouble?'

'Don't know, but Billy needs to speak to me asap.' He walked towards the door.

'You need me to come with you?'

'No, you're all right. You have Amanda Ferguson to deal with.'

Watson knocked on Wright's door and put his head around it. 'Ma'am, sir, I have to nip down and see Billy Clayton in reception. Do you need me?'

'No, we're just discussing details about a possible Ferguson television appeal. Anything we need to know about Billy?' Wright asked.

'Hope not. Seems the Andersons are flexing their muscles. Billy and Davy are in their sights.'

Matthews looked interested. 'I thought they had settled their differences?'

'Woody Anderson wants to be top dog now. I'll keep you posted.' With that, Watson headed down to meet Billy.

'The Thetwell estate is one place we need to deal with,' Matthews said with determination.

'They had a large fire last night,' Wright said.

'I heard, looks like we need to step up patrols on there, especially if a turf war is imminent.'

CHAPTER ELEVEN

A NERVOUS-LOOKING BILLY CLAYTON stood in the police quarter's reception area, reading the information notices about crime.

'Learn anything interesting?' Watson said as he entered the lobby.

'Same old crap you lot put out,' Billy smirked.

'Come in here, we can talk in private.' Watson opened the door to an office off the reception area. Billy walked in and turned to face Watson.

'I'm scared for Davy. He never came home last night.' The expression on Billy's face was one Watson had not seen before. A man who was always confident in what he was doing and saying now looked like a lost boy. Both of them sat down.

Watson was concerned. 'When did you last see him?'

'About seven last night. He had been on edge all weekend, furious with everything and everyone, including me.'

'You don't think he went to deal with the Andersons on his own?'

'Wouldn't put it past him. He's moved to a whole new level in anger since Dad died. I've not seen him like this.'

Watson made some notes. 'Does he still drive that red Vauxhall Vectra?'

Billy nodded. 'Yes, he went out in it last night.'

Watson paused. 'There was a fire over on the Thelwell last night. Do you know anything about that?'

'Yes, I know. The stench is all over the place this morning, and no, I know nothing about it,' Billy exclaimed, shaking his head vehemently.

'Some lock-up went up in flames. Presumed to be owned by the Andersons.'

'And you think Davy had something to do with it?'

'You tell me. Could he have?'

'As I've said, *I don't know*. I hope he didn't.'

Watson saw the fear in Billy's eyes. 'Ok, don't worry I will pass his details across to uniform and ask if they can keep an eye out for him and his car. I will speak to my boss and tell her what's been going on. I don't want this to get out of hand. If I hear anything, I will let you know.'

They exchanged phone numbers before Watson saw Billy out of the station, keeping the door open for a smartly dressed woman and man in a suit who headed straight for the front desk.

When Watson gave the desk sergeant Davy's details, he overheard the name Amanda Ferguson. That must be her father then, Watson thought. He observed the visitors on the way back to the office while they were waiting.

Bumping into Monteith and Sandall as Watson headed back upstairs, he pulled them aside.

'For a woman whose husband was horribly murdered, she looks very composed,' he said.

Monteith nodded. 'That was our impression first time we saw her. Either she's a cold-blooded bitch, or she's a great actress and knows more than she is letting on.'

'Enter the Black Widow,' Sandall added.

'What did Billy want?' Monteith asked, intrigued.

'Davy's gone missing. Stormed out of the house last night and has not been seen since. Billy's worried with the Andersons on the warpath. I have given his details to uniform so they can keep an eye out.'

'God help him if the Andersons grab him first. Billy and Davy need to keep their heads down, and we know that will not happen,' Monteith stated.

Watson nodded as he walked up to the main office, where Matthews was just leaving. 'Amanda Ferguson and her father have just arrived downstairs. Keith and Paul are taking them through to the interview rooms as I speak.'

'Poor woman,' Matthews replied. 'Let's hope our appeals can pick up some information on the killer.'

'There is something not right with her. Both Keith and Paul feel the same,' Watson expressed his reservations.

'What do you mean, Terry?' Wright asked.

'Well, when they went to interview her the first time after she reported him missing, she acted like she couldn't be bothered. But when they went back with Evan's items, she cried for England.'

'Could she be involved?'

Watson shook his head. 'Maybe. Let's see what they come back with after today's interview.'

'We need to be doubly sure it involves her before accusing her of anything,' Matthews reminded them both. 'Keep me updated.'

'Oh, one thing before you leave, sir,' Watson added. 'Davy Clayton's disappeared. Billy came in to report him missing; he's concerned because of the Andersons.'

'That's all we need now. We got rid of the Russells. Now the battle lines are once again drawn,' Matthews remarked annoyed.

'You mentioned you were looking at sorting out the Thelwell Estate,' Wright reminded Matthews. 'This could be the ideal time to do it.'

Watson agreed. 'We could make it look like a raid. Bring in both the Andersons and Claytons and put the frighteners up them.'

Matthews nodded. Watson could see his mind whir around.

'Leave it with me,' Matthews said as he left the office.

'And he will claim he had the idea,' Watson said to Wright once the door was closed.

Woody Anderson and his sons surveyed the debris that used to be one of their garages. The brick walls of the garage were the only things left standing. Inside the brick coffin, the shells of the four burned-out cars. All stolen over the past week. In the backyard, metal cages that held waste stood like a skeleton of twisted wire and metal.

'Do we know if this was deliberate or an accident?' he said through gritted teeth.

'I don't know yet,' Freddie answered grimly. 'I will find out.'

Woody turned to him. 'Make certain you do. What did this lot say?' He waved his hands towards the surrounding houses.

'The first they noticed anything about it was smelling smoke and seeing the flames. No speeding cars or shouts. If it was set on fire, they were in and out fast.'

Woody was seething. He had just lost a third of his motor business. Things like this cost money, time, and effort to set up again. All three he didn't have. Someone had to pay. Any hint of weakness on the estate, there was invariably someone ready to take over. That's why he needed to show the Claytons who the boss was. But had the Claytons struck the first blow?

Speaking aloud, he said, 'I want this mess cleaned up fast.'

'I'm sorry, Mrs Ferguson, Mr Highfield, we have to use one of the interview rooms,' Monteith said as he guided them into the room. 'All our other offices are booked, and this was the only one available.'

Amanda and her dad looked around the small, grey room.

'It's not a problem, detective,' Highfield said as they sat down.

Monteith and Sandall sat down and opened the files in front of them.

Monteith started. 'Thank you again for coming in today. We would like to update you and ask a couple more questions if you feel up to it?'

Amanda looked at her father and nodded.

Was she putting on an act, Monteith wondered.

'I know your father told you how Evan died and where we discovered his body. I won't go over those details again, but I would like to outline for you where we are in the investigation.'

Amanda gripped her father's hand tightly. Both detectives could see her knuckles turn white.

'We have put out an appeal to see if anyone was around the area at the time your husband's car was discovered at Gorges Farm. Whether they spotted Evan's green Saab or overheard an argument. Anything that can help us.' Monteith looked up at Amanda. No change in her demeanour.

He continued, 'The appeal we did in the newspaper came back with nothing conclusive, so we have requested the local radio to put out an appeal today.'

Highfield opened his mouth. 'And if that doesn't come back with anything?'

'If that comes back with nothing,' Monteith looked directly at Amanda, 'we wondered if you felt up to making a TV appeal? You don't have to, but it may help.'

The blood drained from Amanda's face. She shook her head.

'I think it's too early for Amanda to deal with something as big as a TV appeal,' Highfield stated.

'Okay, we just wanted to ask,' Monteith said. 'Could I ask a couple more questions, please?'

'Do you feel up to it?' Highfield asked his daughter.

She nodded. 'Yes.'

'Before you do that though,' Highfield said, 'can I ask, did the owner of this farm see anything?'

'We have his statement. That's all we can say at the moment,' Sandall replied.

Highfield frowned but kept silent.

'Amanda,' Monteith continued. 'Could you tell us a little about you and Evan? We've spoken to his boss at work, Ryan Craven, so we know something about his work life, but it would be helpful to understand how he was at home. Were there any problems?'

Amanda swallowed. 'We had no marriage troubles, detective. We loved each other. Evan was a caring husband.'

The steeliness that both Monteith and Sandall had heard previously was back. It was like she had flipped a switch on.

Who are you protecting? Yourself? Evan? Monteith thought.

'Did Evan socialise with colleagues, or others?'

'Occasionally with colleagues. Mostly, he was at home with me or at work.'

Monteith was growing exasperated. 'You see Amanda, with what happened to Evan, we think he must have done, said, or seen something that pissed someone really off.' He paused for a second. 'Did Evan mention to you any trouble or difficulty he was in?'

Highfield looked concerned as he leaned towards his daughter. 'Amanda, please. If there is anything, tell the detectives. Anything at all.'

Amanda looked at her father. 'I don't know, Daddy. If he was in trouble, he didn't tell me.' She was close to tears. 'Can we go now? I'm getting a migraine.'

Outside the interview room, Highfield stood back and signalled to Monteith. 'I'll have a talk with her when we get back to the house. If she reveals anything, you will be the first to know.'

Monteith thanked him. 'That's my direct phone number. Please call if you need anything.'

He walked them out and then went up to the office.

'How was our little actress?' Watson asked.

Monteith sat in his chair. 'It's like she has two personalities, one vulnerable and the other very confident. She switched between them effortlessly.'

'That is it your professional opinion, Dr Monteith?' Watson joked,

'No, is it heck. She's playing us, *that* I'm sure of. She's covering for someone. Either she knows why Evan was killed or someone told her to stay silent. She even refused to do the TV appeal. Her dad said it was too soon, but he will talk to her. Maybe he will change her mind.'

'I don't give it much hope,' Watson sighed, looking at his watch. 'The appeal on the local radio went out over the last hour. Fingers crossed we hear something from the public. Dashcam footage wouldn't go amiss. Paul, did we get everything from traffic cams the night of the fire?'

Paul reached over for the reports. 'No nothing, there aren't many out there. The ones that were, were out due to maintenance.'

'Typical,' Monteith said exasperated. 'They watch over you like Big Brother, but the moment we need them, they aren't working.'

'Boss, I think we have something,' French called. She had been keeping tabs on the phones and anything reported via Crimestoppers. Watson and Monteith looked up and walked over to her desk.

'Somebody rang in earlier saying he nearly got sideswiped by a 4x4 on the same night near Gorge Farm. Said he was travelling out of the city when a dark blue 4x4 almost hit him at a junction heading back into the city. Said it was driving erratically. He didn't get a registration number, unfortunately, but does have a dashcam. He noticed also that it had four people in it.'

'Did the caller leave a name and number?'

'Let Emma and Karl check that out. I have something else for you to look at,' Wright said from the doorway of her office. 'Come in here, both of you.'

As Monteith and Watson sat down in Wright's office, she handed a couple of sheets to Watson. 'That is the visitor's list from HMP Rightwell. Check who visited your old boss.'

Watson flicked through the pages before spotting a familiar name. 'Elizabeth Preston?'

Wright nodded. 'The day before Kenneth Crompton took his life.'

'You think she said something that sent him over the edge?' Monteith asked.

'Yes, that's possible. I want you two to see her and ask about the visit.'

———

The front door slammed shut on Nigel Highfield. The ride back from the police headquarters had been frosty at best. Amanda, no matter how hard he had asked, didn't want to talk about Evan's death and her attitude during the interview. He felt something was not right, even though he understood she'd rather not have her life scrutinised on television.

Emily opened the door. She looked surprised. 'What happened? She just walked in and shot straight upstairs. What happened at the station?'

As they were talking, they heard the front door open and slam shut again. Rushing to the window, they saw Amanda jump into her car and drive off at full speed.

'Where the bloody hell is she going?'

—

Joey was examining the underside of the Porsche he was working on as his phone beeped. A text message. Wiping his hands, he pulled the phone out to see who had called.

We need to meet urgently. Usual place.

CHAPTER TWELVE

'W‍HAT DID YOU FIND out?' Woody Anderson asked Freddie as he joined him at the table.

The Andersons were in the rear room of their local, The Cross Keys, taking stock of their businesses. All illegal. The fire at the garage had been a blow, leaving them short of stock, premises, and, most importantly, income.

Freddie took a mouthful of his beer. 'Definitely arson,' he replied as he placed his glass down. 'Started out the back amongst the wastepaper and cardboard. Spread to the building rapidly. I told Speedy to get that backyard cleared the other day. Now, this has happened.'

Woody slammed his fist on the table. 'Where is he now?'

'Helping with the cleanup.'

'I want to see him later.' His expression was grim.

Freddie nodded to Luke, who laughed before walking out with Andrew.

'You think he did it?' Freddie asked his dad.

'No. He doesn't have the brains, never mind the bottle to do this. He's good as a car thief and with the converting. Not arson.'

'The Claytons?'

Woody clammed his mouth shut and peered at Freddie.

Freddie took another mouthful of beer and shook his head. 'If they pulled this off, they either have big balls or a death wish.'

Woody nodded. 'I hope we haven't underestimated the two Clayton punks.' He pondered and added, his voice steely, 'And if they set our shed ablaze, they will pay for it.'

James McGill, attired in a sharp suit, appeared at the door to Ryan Craven's office, who was deep in conversation with one of the mechanics.

Craven clocked his guest. 'Give us a minute,' he asked the mechanic. 'I will look at it later.'

McGill shut the door behind him and made himself comfortable on one of the tatty chairs.

'What do you want? I'm busy,' Ryan said, turning to the computer.

'That's not friendly, Ryan. I expected more courtesy from you. I need you to drive for a visit I've planned tonight.'

'Me?'

McGill looked around. 'I don't see anyone else in this office. Yes, you.'

Craven's hand trembled as he picked up some papers. 'Why not Travis, or any of your other drivers?'

McGill got up and stood close to Craven, breathing in his ear. 'They are coming with you.'

Craven turned to face McGill. 'Where?' he muttered.

'The farmer. He spoke to the police and needs a lesson.'

Craven's eyes shifted. 'What? I can't believe... You've got to be joking. Dealing with Evan the way you did was one thing. But the farmer? You're asking us to do what? Beat him up?'

McGill grinned. 'A lesson, I said. I've given Travis the orders. You're to drive them over and do whatever he tells you to do. Got it? Be ready at nine tonight.' He flung open the door and marched out.

Craven fell back in his chair, shaking all over. He threw his head in his hands and just sat there.

Joey popped his head in. 'What did the royal nastiness want?'

Craven looked up, terror in his eyes. 'For us to do his dirty work again.'

'I might have some more bad news. Amanda just texted and said she wants to meet urgently.'

'Did she say why?'

'No, but she met those detectives this morning. Could have something to do with that.'

Craven grabbed his jacket. 'I'm coming with you this time.'

Davy turned the key in the front door and stepped inside. Last night had been a blur of drink, drugs, and partying. His hangover was big; he was lucky the police hadn't pulled him over. Even at lunchtime, he would still have tested positive for both drink and drugs.

Avoiding the police was one thing. Avoiding his brother another.

'Where the hell have you been?' Billy yelled from the kitchen. 'I've been worried.'

'Out having fun,' Davy replied as he pushed past his brother into the kitchen. He grabbed a glass and opened the fridge for a bottle of beer.

'You stink of booze. Are those leftovers of drugs on your shirt? Jesus!' Billy ranted.

Davy sat at the table and opened the bottle. 'Don't you start! You're turning into dad. I had enough of this from him.'

'And he was right. Kept you from going off the rails at an early age. If it wasn't for him, where would you be?'

'In a better place than here,' Davy snapped.

Billy seethed. He grabbed Davy's glass and poured it down the kitchen sink. 'You've had enough.'

Davy launched himself at Billy, fists flying hitting him both in the head and body. Billy retaliated with punches to Davy's body. flying,Neither brother would let up. Years of pent-up anger within Davy rushed out like an avalanche, and Billy was on the receiving end. Punches rained down on him, his already broken nose took its fair share, blood spurting out everywhere.

The fight moved into the living room. Billy, covering up from Davy's punches, got a rapid one-two into Davy's body which took the wind out of him. This gave Billy the chance to retaliate by sticking a couple of punches in Davy's face. The cut above his right eye sprang open again and blood flowed everywhere.

Watson and Monteith stood by Monteith's BMW as they stared over the road to The Dragon's Den. It looked derelict and was boarded up, with a "For Sale" sign attached to the wall where the pub's sign used to be.

'You're about a month too late for last orders,' a neighbour washing his car shouted.

'Any idea where the owners moved to?' Monteith asked, walking across the road and showing his ID.

'Nope. It was open the last weekend in July, and then it didn't open again. The brewery came and put that for sale sign up a couple of days after. Didn't see them move out. Which was a pain because they owed my wife wages, she was a cleaner.'

'There was no inkling that they would close so suddenly?' Watson asked.

'No. One day open, the next closed. What are you asking for?'

'Just needed to talk to them. No worries, thanks for the information.' They walked back to Monteith's car.

'So, what do you think happened?' Monteith said as he put his seat belt on and started the engine.

'My guess would be that Elizabeth went to Crompton and told him she was leaving. That sent him over the edge. All the trouble he went to in killing her brother's murderer in revenge, and she turns around and tells him she is buggering off.'

'And he realises that everything he had done is for nothing. Thrown away his career, his life, and family.'

'Or she couldn't stay in the place where her brother was murdered and had to move for sanity's sake.'

'Hopefully, we'll find out,' said Monteith. 'By the way, I can still smell the aftermath of the fire.'

Watson wound up his window. 'You're right.'

They drove past the boarding hostel for released prisoners. In the car park at the front stood the manager, Sheila Evans, with a couple of builders looking at the demolished front wall. Monteith pulled over.

'Hi, Sheila, had problems?' Watson asked.

'Some joyrider crashed through it last night, and left a front bumper.' Sheila bent down and picked up a long thick piece of black plastic. Broken bits hung off it and the scrub marks were plain to see. 'And me with a large bill for the rebuild of this wall. Luckily, the council will have to foot it.'

'Have you reported it?' Monteith asked.

Sheila came across and stood by the car, looking through Watson's window. 'Yes, straight after it happened but as always nothing came off it. I don't know why I bother.'

'What's the word on the street about last night's fire?' Watson tentatively asked, unsure if Sheila would comment.

She glanced around furtively before leaning down.

'Word is, it was an Anderson premise that went up. Don't know if it was arson but rumours are flying around. Not that I said anything,' she hastily added as she turned back to the builders.

As Monteith pulled away from the curb, he spotted two teenagers taking a long look at them and the hostel from in front of the corner shop. 'Wonder who they are lookouts for?' Monteith commented as he drove slowly by, staring at them.

'We can ask Billy when we get there.'

Silently, they drove into the street where the Clayton brothers lived. Neighbours had gathered on the pavement.

'What the hell is going on?' Monteith exclaimed as he shut down the car.

Jumping out of the car, Watson and Monteith shot up the driveway past Davy's car and hammered on the door.

'How long has this been going on for?' Monteith shouted at a man standing on the front grass.

'About ten minutes, mate. They're going hell for leather at each other in there. Shall we call the police?'

They heard breaking glass. The front window smashed showering the men in glass as a small bronze statue flew past their heads. They heard furniture being broken and heavy swearing.

'Enough,' said Watson. 'Come on, Keith, get that door,' He stood aside as Monteith ran at the door and karate kicked it. The door frame splintered as the lock went. Charging in, they found Billy backed into a corner of the living room with Davy waving a knife around.

Monteith launched himself at Davy, knocking him off balance. The knife came out of his hand and landed on the floor. Davy made a grab for it but Monteith was quicker and took Davy down face first on the floor, putting the handcuffs on.

Billy, face covered in blood from his re-broken nose, made a run for it, but Watson grabbed him and threw him on the sofa. 'Stay there,' he bellowed.

Two uniformed officers appeared through the front door and helped Monteith haul Davy, who was kicking and screaming, off the floor.

'I'm fucking going to kill the lot of you,' Davy hollered, kicking at anything and everyone, just missing Watson's legs.

Monteith stood in front of him. 'Davy Clayton, you are under arrest for possession of an offensive weapon, assault, and that's just for starters. Get him out of here.'

The officers, each holding one of Davy's arms, struggled to get him out of the house.

Watson looked around the room. Smashed furniture, blood spatters all over the walls and floor. He sighed and turned to Billy, who had slumped down on the sofa. 'Looks like you two had a knockout fight. What the hell started it?'

'Billy turned up drunk and smelling of drugs. I challenged him over where he had been, and he just hit the roof. Accused me of being like dad.'

'You know we have to take you in as well?'

'What? In my car? With him spurting blood everywhere?' Monteith protested. 'Not likely.'

'I'm sure Billy will pay for valeting if he drips over your back seat,' Watson grinned.

Amanda Ferguson sat on a bench in the central park. She nervously looked around the pathways, scanning the faces for Joey. The interview at the police station had not gone the way she hoped it would. She hadn't coped well. And just mentioning going on TV had set internal alarm bells ringing. If her father hadn't taken over then, who knows... Would she have blurted everything out there and then? She'd felt like it. What had Evan got them into? No, wait. Ryan Craven had got them into something dangerous. Something that'd cost her husband's life. Who else would be next?

Looking to her left, she spotted Joey walking towards her. Her heart sank when she recognised Craven with him. She wanted to run, get away from everything.

Joey held his arms open, approaching Amanda. She glared. 'Sorry Amanda, he wanted to come.'

'What do you want?' she said scornfully.

'Let's move somewhere more private, please?' Craven took Amanda's arm.

'No, let's not,' she stood firm. 'I only asked Joey to meet up. What the hell are you doing here?'

Craven held her arm tightly.

'Let go, you're hurting me,' Amanda exclaimed.

Passers-by looked up. Craven let go.

Leaning into her and Joey, Craven lowered his voice. 'There will be a lot more pain to come for all of us if you don't.' He walked towards a more secluded area of the park.

Amanda stared at Joey, who nodded. 'Just go with him. Things have developed and not for the better.'

Craven found an empty picnic table, away from prying eyes. Sitting down, he instructed Amanda and Joey to sit opposite him.

Twenty yards away, Nigel Highfield was observing the three of them. He had followed his daughter to the park after she had left the house in a hurry. Something had been nagging him, but he couldn't put his finger on it. His carefree daughter had changed into someone he didn't recognise. His wife suggested it was part of the grieving process, but Nigel felt there was more.

Looking at his daughter with two men he hadn't seen before, he realised his concerns were founded. What was Amanda up to? What had Evan been up to, to get him killed in that horrible way? Things didn't add up. Slowly but deliberately, he strolled over.

'Hello darling. Are you going to introduce me to your friends?'

CHAPTER THIRTEEN

THE TEENAGE BOY RAN as hard as he could. They had given him the task of passing on a message. Word had spread throughout the estate, and the teenager was the last in line to tell the people who needed to know. Rounding the corner at full pelt he misjudged his speed and crashed into a low wall, flying over it. Picking himself up, he held his arm and looked down at his ripped jeans. A small price to pay.

The boy limped into the Cross Keys pub, still holding his arm. Finding who he needed to speak to, he passed on his information. A ten-pound note was stuffed into the boy's hand. Luke left the table and walked into the back room. Woody and Freddie were holding court with Speedy. Spotting Luke, Woody cut short the conversation.

Luke grinned. 'The Claytons have been arrested. Davy went mental and assaulted Billy.'

Woody smiled broadly. 'Time to move.'

It was getting late. The last thing Watson and Monteith wanted was to deal with was the feuding Clayton brothers, but alas, that's what was on the menu now. They had Billy in one interview room and Davy in a separate one, still handcuffed and with two officers looking after him.

Davy had been kicking off in the police cells. The officers who brought him in had their work cut out getting him out of the police van and into the station. Davy was aggressive and not in the mood for cooperation. It took five officers to get him in through the door. There was no way he would answer questions, cursing and swearing at the duty officer. They soon gave up and brought him back to his cell.

Billy, on the other hand, was as quiet as a mouse.

Both were on the way down to start the interviews as PC Gary Kendall caught up with them.

'Thought you may want to see this before interviewing the Claytons.' He handed over a file. 'Just been confirmed.'

Watson opened the file, read it, and passed it to Monteith. 'Are they certain it was arson?'

'A hundred per cent, accelerant found at the scene.'

'Thanks, Gary.'

They walked into the interview room. Billy came clean to them. He told Watson and Monteith what took place when Davy got home.

Watson opened the file on the desk. 'Davy said he was at a friend's house before coming home this morning. Did he say which friend and where?'

'No, he just said he was out having fun. I could smell from the stink of drink and drugs.'

'So, he didn't say where he'd been?' Watson pressed.

'No, why?'

Watson and Monteith glanced at each other before Watson continued.

'Billy, do you recall when you came in to report Davy missing?'

Billy looked confused. 'Yes, why?'

'On the same night, there was a fire at a workshop on the Anderson side of the estate. We now know it was arson.'

Billy managed a double take between Watson and Monteith. 'And you think Davy did it?'

'Is it possible? He has been threatening the Andersons. Did he say anything to you?'

Billy took his time before providing an answer. 'No, he hasn't. True, we have argued over what to do. The Andersons have tried to intimidate us. But we decided that if they want us out, let them make the first move.'

Watson phrased his next question carefully. 'So, would Davy in his present state set fire to Anderson's garage?'

Billy shrugged. 'Who knows? You've seen how he has been. If he did it, I knew nothing about it.'

They closed the interview and went to fetch Davy.

Davy was still wound up. 'When are you going to release me? I'll plead guilty to possession of a knife and fighting so just release me on bail and I'll go to court.'

'Maybe, but first tell us where you were from Sunday evening until we entered your house, Davy?' asked Monteith.

Davy shrugged. 'I can't remember.'

'According to Billy, you said, "Out having fun," Where was that?'

Davy shrugged again.

Monteith turned to Watson. 'We could always do a drug and alcohol test, Davy?'

'You can't do that!' Davy blurted out.

'That sounds like a cracking idea,' Watson said to Monteith, ignoring Davy's protestations.

'No. You... You...'

Monteith made a point of sniffing the air. 'I can smell it on you. If you were driving last night and this morning, bang goes your licence.'

Davy just shook his head.

'Thought not,' Monteith said. 'So, out with it. Where were you?'

Davy grinned. 'I think I'll have the duty solicitor now.'

Ryan Craven slowly eased the van down the lane leading to Gorge Farm. This was not where he wanted to be, but the consequences of not taking part didn't bear thinking about. Even though he had been doing that since yesterday afternoon.

With him were Greatbatch and Whiteman, McGill's go-to men. He feared both.

Low clouds cut out most of the light from the night sky as he inched the van past the large barn where they had set fire to Evan Ferguson. Craven cut the main headlights using only the sidelights as they approached the farmhouse. Henson's Land Rover and Corsa were parked next to each other in front of the farm.

He parked up, switching off the lights and engine. They studied the house for the next five minutes, checking for movement. There were no lights on.

Greatbatch leaned over. 'Leave the keys in the ignition for a quick getaway.'

The three of them climbed out and opened the rear doors.

Whiteman nodded at Craven. 'Have a glance around. We will sort this lot out.'

'Why me?'

'Because I said so, and I'm in charge. GOT IT?'

Craven shut up. He had to obey. He didn't hang around and set off to the farmhouse while Whiteman and Greatbatch were laughing. God, he *had* to get away from all of this somehow. He could take off over the nearby fields, but run where? They would find him soon enough. Checking around the single-story farmhouse was brief and easy. There were no gates or fences, just a path leading around it. The back garden had a large vegetable plot and a couple of flower beds by the back door. He glimpsed through a couple of windows, seeing no lights or movement inside, before making his way back to the evil twins.

'All clear, no lights on, looks like they're in bed.'

'Excellent, here take these,' Whiteman ordered as he handed Craven a crowbar and a couple of crude petrol bombs.

'What? I was told just to drive you here. Nobody said anything about taking part.' Craven felt alarmed.

Greatbatch smirked. 'Change of plans. Orders from the boss.'

They moved to the house. Standing by the front door, Whiteman issued a final, simple order. 'Pick a window, crowbar it open, and lob a petrol bomb in.'

Craven looked at Whiteman and Greatbatch. *I don't want to do this*, he thought, desperate now.

'Go on Craven, you first,' Whiteman said coldly, swinging a crowbar in his hand.

Approaching the nearest window, Craven put the bomb down before tackling the window. The wooden frame split easily, releasing the lock and catch. He eased the window wide. Before he could throw the petrol bomb, he was stopped by Whiteman's crowbar. It was smashed against his skull. His head split.

Whiteman and Greatbatch picked Craven's lifeless body up and shoved it through the open window, followed by a couple of lighted petrol bombs. The room disappeared in flame and smoke as the petrol spread, covering the floor and all the furniture.

Greatbatch used his crowbar on the window on the other side of the front door and threw in a couple more petrol bombs. Whiteman took care of the Land Rover and the Corsa. When finished, they ran to the van.

Greatbatch slammed the van into gear and floored it. Branches snapped off the overhanging hedges either side of the lane as the van careered down back to the main road. Turning onto it, Greatbatch slowed down to the speed limit. He glanced at Whiteman. Job done.

Tuesday

Billy eased his battered and bruised body out of the police car and onto his own drive. His body was screaming for painkillers. Even though it was the middle of the night, somebody had already boarded up the smashed front window and door. Great neighbours, he thought. Steven Williams was one of those. Spotting Billy getting out of the taxi, he caught up with him as Billy tried the front door, explaining that the smashed window and door were to be replaced in the morning for free. You look after your neighbours; they look after you.

Inside was still a wreck. Billy cleared the debris off the unbroken sofa and they both sat down with a strong drink. Billy took Steven through what went on down at the station.

'We've got more pressing matters to deal with,' Steven said. 'After your arrest, news spread fast. Woody Anderson went on the offensive. You might not know this, but when your pa was ill, the Andersons tried to get some men to swap sides. Woody welcomed them with open arms,' Steven paused. 'Now, with this fight between you and Davy... that sealed the deal. They don't want to work for you anymore.'

Billy threw his glass at the wall in frustration and anger. He bristled with indignation.

'I'll let myself out and sort the window and front door,' Steven said as he got up. 'Be seeing you, man.'

Billy sat down, nursing another drink and his thoughts. Was it time to throw in the towel? Did he have the balls to continue what his father had set up? Davy had grown into more of a handicap than a help. Had he set fire to Anderson's garage?

Washed and changed, after barely five hours of sleep, Billy set about clearing and cleaning the wreck of a house. Opening the front room curtains, he faced the carnage that they had done to their home. Last night it didn't register, even when he had sat in it with

Steven. Seeing it in the cold light of day, Billy took it all in. The smashed front window, the broken door. Blood splatters up the wall and over the carpet. Chairs turned over and ornaments that their father had collected smashed. He found the glass he smashed last night in a fit of rage Fetching a bin liner, he began the clean-up with that glass.

A knock on the door made him look up. Steven was outside with his workmates to get started on the new window and door. He waved them in as the phone went. The duty solicitor told Billy Davy's court appearance would be at two p.m. He explained he'd not attend. Davy had burned his bridges, and Billy refused to be on the receiving end of his brother's fury anymore.

As soon as he put his mobile down, it was ringing again. He knew the number. Billy was in no frame of mind for pleasantries. 'Anderson, what the fuck do you want?'

'And good morning to you too, Billy.'

'Piss off.'

'I understood there was a disagreement at the latest board meeting of Claytons Limited,' Anderson laughed.

'Just get to the point, Anderson. I'm busy.'

Hearing the name Anderson, Steven looked up. He came inside and stood next to Billy.

'Seems the rats are leaving the sinking ship and turning to me for protection. Your business on this estate is dead.'

'I heard you were picking up our crap workers. You can have them for all I care. Shows what type of people they are if they're going to work for you, Anderson. Trash goes where the deepest bin is.'

Anderson laughed again. 'Trash? Is that why Davy is in front of the courts today? Give up Clayton, you have had your time. Let the bigger boys run this estate and you two can disappear and play with your toys.'

'Fuck off,' Billy shouted as he ended the call.

Steven stared at Billy. 'I take it that was a courtesy call from Woody Anderson.'

'Yes. He needs to brush up his bedside manners.'

Steven placed a hand on Billy's shoulder. 'Let's get this all fixed up first. I think it's time for a war meeting.'

Gorge Farm was nothing more than a shell. Firefighters had been there throughout the early hours of the morning bringing the fire under control and dampening it down.. It was only now at eight o'clock after the fire chief had briefed them, that the SOCO team, Lorimer, French, and Mac could begin their examination.

Arson with one casualty, the fire chief had declared.

'Someone was inside. I thought the Hensons had left for a few days,' French said after the debrief.

'They have,' Lorimer confirmed. 'Moved down to Brighton to stay with their son and his family, or we might have three bodies for Mac to deal with.'

Mac just grinned as he and Chris Stocks, the SOCO team leader, headed for the farmhouse.

'So, who do we have in there then?' French wondered.

'The arsonist? Someone who stumbled on whoever started the fire and paid the cost? One thing I can bet on, this was another warning from whoever killed Evan Ferguson.'

'For talking to us?'

'Definitely. Henson told us they'd warned him. When the appeal went out, we put him right in their sights.'

Putting on protective clothing, they joined Mac and Stocks in the shell of a house.

Joey turned into the Barton Industrial Estate and parked up in front of Craven Autos. One of the mechanics was opening up. Usually, Ryan would be in early and open up.

Joey knew there was a chance Ryan would be late today.

CHAPTER FOURTEEN

THE CID OFFICE WAS buzzing with activity when two leading officers from the county drug unit arrived, informing them they were looking into drug couriers in Ravenswood. They were in with Matthews to brief him about the operation.

'They're all we need!' Monteith said, exasperated. 'We've already got so much on our plate and now this lot wants help.'

DSI Wright called the office to order. 'We will handle the drug unit when they see fit to include us. Before that, we have our own investigations. The Hensons have been contacted by the Sussex police, and have been told to stay there for the time being.'

'Are we linking it to the Ferguson murder?' Sandall asked.

'Absolutely,' stated Watson. 'It's too much of a coincidence not to link it.'

Wright nodded. 'I agree. It was a good job the son talked his parents into taking some time off down in Brighton, or we would be looking at a multiple murder scene.'

'Which brings us to the next question. Whose body was found in the ashes?' Sandall asked.

'I take it either Karl or Emma have been in contact with an update?' Wright asked.

'Came off the phone with Karl just before coming in,' Watson confirmed. 'Arson according to the fire chief. It destroyed the farmhouse and both their cars. They found one male individual inside the house. Mac will take the body back with him once the SOCO team has finished.'

'Was anybody looking after the farm while they were away?' Monteith asked.

'No,' Sandall replied. 'They lived alone. After they left, the uniformed presence was stood down. No need to keep a check on an empty house.'

'Anything come back from the dashcam footage we were given?' Wright asked.

'Nothing much. It shows four vehicles on the road about a quarter of a mile away from Henson's farm. Two were cars, but the other two were larger vehicles. One was a dark 4x4, so could be our getaway one. Need the tech bods to enhance the pictures to check. There are no streetlights out there so it's hard to make out details.'

'Can you see to that now, Paul?' Watson asked. 'We need to know if it's useful.'

Sandall went to his desk just as Chief Superintendent Matthews appeared in the main office with the two drug officers.

'Ok, before we get interrupted,' Wright said, looking in Matthews' direction, causing Watson and Monteith to turn their heads, 'are we on the verge of gang warfare?'

'I hope not,' Watson replied, 'but Davy is behaving like a one-man wrecking ball. That's why we had them both in here last night.'

Monteith agreed. 'Davy is the loose cannon, he's on a crash course to take Woody Anderson head-on. He's already tried to punch the man's lights out and we are looking into whether he set fire to the Anderson's garage.'

Matthews appeared at Wright's door with the two drug officers. 'Can we interrupt?'

'Give us a couple of minutes, sir. We are discussing the Thelwell Estate,' Wright said.

'Oh, I'll sit in if you don't mind.' Matthew ushered in his two guests and stood by the back wall. 'Don't mind us.'

Wright looked annoyed. Watson looked at Monteith and rolled his eyes.

'Ok, right,' continued Wright. 'We have previously talked to the Claytons. I need you two,' she looked at Watson and Monteith, 'to speak to the Andersons. Tell them we are watching them.'

'Great,' Monteith exclaimed. 'Go into the lion's den when he is sharpening his claws.'

Matthews' voice sounded harsh. 'You *will* see Woody Anderson.'

'Can I borrow your car then? I'm not taking mine onto that side of the estate,' Monteith grumbled.

'Detective Inspector Monteith,' Wright raised her voice. 'Cool it.'

Watson pulled on Monteith's sleeve and both men went to leave Wright's office. Mathews stopped them short.

'Can you two stay? We may call for your input. I'd like to introduce DCI Leon Costa and DI Oliver Underwood of the county drug unit. They would like our help in an operation they're running on our patch.'

———

McGill strode into Craven Autos like he owned the place. After searching in the office and finding no one in there, he shouted, 'Where's Ryan?'

'He's not arrived yet,' Joey, who was lowering the ramp with the Porsche he was working on, responded. 'Can I help you?'

'When he does, tell him I need to speak to him.' McGill turned and strode back across to his own business.

Joey looked at the clock on the wall by the office. Almost noon. *Where are you, Ryan?* He had twice rung his phone, to no avail. Walking into the office, he tried for the third time. Still nothing.

He was worried and scared. Gathering himself together, he finally sent the text message he hoped he wouldn't have to.

> URGENT Ryan not at work, no answer on his phone, arrange the meeting

———

The Royal Oak pub was the watering hole for everybody on the Claytons' side of the estate. This lunchtime, the owner closed it for an emergency session. The locals had come to terms with missing out on their pints. Most were at the gathering anyway.

Inside were the heads of the families still supporting the Claytons ordered to attend by Billy and Steven Williams.

Billy addressed the special gathering, updating them on everything that had happened since the death of Joseph.

Some families who had lived on the estate as long as the Claytons and had seen the boys grow up voiced their concerns about Davy. Billy listened to them. He needed their support, just as much as his father had their backing back then.

If the Andersons wanted to take over the estate, they wouldn't get it without a fight.

A MOMENTOUS FIGHT.

'Did they suspect anything?' Travis Whiteman asked McGill.

'Nothing. That little squirt Joey said Ryan was not in, so I just said I needed to speak to him.'

'Do you think he told anyone about last night?'

'No. The only thing he knew was that he was driving for you two, that's all. So, what is he going to say?' McGill was in his usual self-indulgent mood. 'Anyway, we have more important things to talk about. Have the parcels gone out today?'

'Yes, they're on Greatbatch's and Adams' vans today,' Whiteman confirmed. 'Shaun has delivered his, but Adams has still to report back. He was going the furthest though. Should be delivered by two p.m.'

'Good, Adams is the crucial one. We almost fucked up that delivery sending that useless pillock, Ferguson. Tell me why?' McGill stared at Whiteman.

'Because we had no one else to deliver. Both Greatbatch and Adams were busy, and you didn't trust any of our other drivers.

Craven suggested Ferguson because he would keep his trap shut. And if you didn't send anybody with the packages, then it would've been either of us in that car instead of Ferguson. The bosses wanted blood. Ferguson was the fall guy.'

'Don't remind me,' McGill exclaimed. 'I got hauled over the coals by the big bosses because of that. They were not happy. That on top of not getting the deliveries out on time when that jerk crashed that car the other month. My card has been well and truly marked.'

'That wasn't your fault. That was the police shutting the whole estate.'

'Try telling them that.'

Sandall was refilling his mug with coffee as Lorimer and French returned from Gorge Farm.

'All I'm saying is you should take Mac up on his offer. What's the problem?' a frustrated French said as she put her bag and coat down.

'No. Not doing it. End of story.' Lorimer threw his car keys and jacket on his desk and grabbed his mug.

'What's Mac offering?' Sandall asked.

'Mac had offered Karl a chance to see the post-mortem on our deceased friend from Gorge Farm after I told Mac that he had not seen one before,' Emma said.

Lorimer took French's cup and moved over to Sandall. 'And I said no way I would set foot in the morgue.'

'There's nothing to it, Karl,' Sandall smiled. 'You're not in the room. You're watching from the overhead balcony when Mac strips and cuts the body before reaching in and taking out the person's vital organs for investigating and weighing. And that's before he saws open the skull and removes the brain.'

'You're a sod sometimes, Paul Sandall.' Lorimer sounded annoyed. 'Anyway, where is everybody?'

'In there,' Sandall nodded. 'The county drug unit wants our help in an operation. Matthews is in there as well.'

'Matthews? Must be serious. Any ideas?'

'No. I'm chasing up the tech bods for the dashcam footage from the original cremation at Gorge Farm. Hang on. It's just come in.' Sandall opened the email as Lorimer and French gathered around.

Attached to the email was a full dashcam recording of the road as the owner passed Gorge Farm. It lasted about ten seconds. 'The owner of the recording said four vehicles passed in the other direction. Two cars, one van, and a 4x4. The 4x4 was being driven erratically and solely on sidelights,' Sandall commented. Below the recording were four blown-up pictures of the front of each vehicle, number plates included. None of them was readable.

Sandall increased the resolution on his computer to read the number plates, writing down what he could make out. 'The first car looks like a Seat Leon, number plate AG 17 SKM. The van's last three letters are PSA. The second car is a Mercedes; the plate reads LC 18. I can't make out the last three letters. The 4x4 is a Toyota Land Cruiser, CD 04 DSC.'

French looked at the information boards. 'Didn't SOCO say the getaway vehicle could be a Land Cruiser?'

'Yes,' Sandall confirmed as he watched the footage again, pausing the recording when the 4x4 appeared. 'I can't tell how many are in this 4x4, two definitely in the front, but whether there's anyone in the back, I don't know.'

Monteith's desk phone rang. Lorimer leant over and answered. 'DI Monteith's phone, DS Lorimer speaking.'

Sandall joined French at the information boards and added the vehicles and their number plates from the dashcam footage. 'I will check with DVLA and our Automatic Number Plate Recognition database. The Land Cruiser first.'

'Keith is in a meeting, but Paul may be available. I will check to see if anyone can come down. Cheers.'

'I'm available for what?' Sandall asked.

'Interesting,' Lorimer said after putting the phone down. 'That was the front desk asking for you and Keith. Seems we have Amanda Ferguson, her father, and their solicitor downstairs.'

DCI Costa and DI Underwood from the Counties Drug Unit were the centre of attention in one of the larger side rooms of the CID main office.

Costa gave the overview. 'We noticed a London drug gang sending drugs around this area and surrounding counties. They have moved away from transporting the drugs in cars up and down the motorways and have picked a more direct way in which they can move a lot more in one go.'

'Has this anything to do with county lines drug runs?' Monteith was the first to ask the obvious question.

'No, not as such,' Underwood clarified. 'You might think so because the drugs we are talking about come from London via other cities. But county line operators drive out local dealers and use mainly children and youngsters as their runners. We're talking about the use of non-conspicuous parcel delivery vans here. The gang we are after supplies drugs to the rich and highflyers in your area. High-class heroin, cocaine, and whatever else they request.'

'I've seen in the reports your figures for drug busts have gone up again,' Costa added.

'Sadly, yes,' Wright confirmed. 'It's a double-edged sword. We raid places and arrest the dealers, but with the low sanctions, they could be out dealing again in months. And while they are inside, a new wave of dealers takes their place.'

Costa nodded. 'I know. It feels we are fighting a losing battle, which is why we want your help with this operation.'

'Anything you need we will provide,' Matthews stated firmly.

'Thank you,' Costa said. 'The Met police have been covertly watching this gang from London for the last year. As I said, they transport their drugs via parcel delivery firms, all boxed and packed up to look like orders from manufacturers or shops.'

Watson glanced at Monteith. This was interesting.

'They deliver their pallets and parcels to a central hub in London, where they are shipped out by trunkers to area hubs in the country. The Met has had people working at the central London hub collecting intelligence.'

'Sorry, but what's a trunker?' Monteith asked puzzled.

'The name trunker comes from the way they are transported. Long-distance freight HGVs using motorways, or so-called trunk roads,' Underwood explained.

Monteith was impressed. 'You learn something every day.'

Costa continued, 'From the area hub in Cambridge, the trunker delivers the parcels and pallets to a local depot. The one for this area is in Ravenswood. We have had our people working at the area hub for the last few months, and now the call has come from London to put an end to this and raid the outlying depots. Ravenswood included.'

'Which delivery firm are we looking at?' Wright asked.

'Wild West Deliveries is the main one for this area.'

Watson couldn't stop a grin on his face. Monteith smiled broadly.

'Got the bastard,' Watson exclaimed.

Costa and Underwood looked perplexed. 'You've had dealings with Wild West Deliveries?'

'Oh yes,' Matthews said. 'Specifically, with the owner, one James McGill.' He turned to Watson and Monteith. 'I thought you would enjoy that. It's why I wanted you in on the briefing.'

"Thank you," Watson said, still smiling. 'You have made our day. James McGill has been a thorn in our side for a long time and it will be good to wipe that smug smile off his face.'

'I understand. Your boss brought us up to date. He sounds like a real bastard.'

'The biggest you've ever seen,' Watson grinned. 'I'm going to enjoy this.'

'Ok, you have our support and resources. How do you want to do this?' Wright asked Costa.

Before he could explain, there was a knock on the door, and Sandall entered. 'Sorry to bother you. Just had a phone call from the front desk. Amanda Ferguson, her father, and their solicitor are downstairs wanting urgently to speak to DI Monteith and me.'

CHAPTER FIFTEEN

'I WONDER WHICH AMANDA Ferguson we will have today,' Monteith said sarcastically as they headed for the stairs. 'The tearful grieving widow or the "I can't be bothered" widow.'

'Whichever it is, DI Monteith, you will behave accordingly,' Matthews, who was entering the lift, said firmly. 'Her husband was murdered, so unless she is a suspect, you keep your opinions to yourself.' With that, the lift doors closed.

Sandall grinned. 'Consider yourself told off.'

Monteith cursed under his breath. 'Let's get this over with. I want to get home at a decent time this evening.'

They walked down to the reception area and took Amanda, her father, and their solicitor into an interview room. They sat down and Sandall started the recording tapes and interview procedure.

'Amanda, do you have any more information that will help us catch your husband's killer?'

She nodded. 'Yes, I know who killed my husband and Ryan Craven.'

Sandall and Monteith glanced at each other.

'Just to clarify, you believe Ryan Craven is dead?' Monteith asked.

'Yes. Joey told me this morning he had not turned up for work.'

'And what makes you and Joey think Ryan is dead?'

'Because yesterday he told us he was to drive James McGill's right-hand men, Shaun Greatbatch and Travis Whiteman, over to Gorge Farm. This morning, Joey said that Shaun and Travis were working at Mc Gill's delivery firm, but Ryan had not turned up.'

Monteith paused. 'Gorge Farm. You're sure that's where they were going?'

'Yes,' Amanda stated firmly.

Monteith nodded as he stole another look at Sandall. Clearly, Amanda had realised she had to stop putting on an act and work with them to catch her husband's murderer.

'And you said you know who killed Evan?'

Amanda looked Monteith straight in the eyes. 'James McGill, Shaun Greatbatch, and Travis Whiteman.'

Back in the office, Watson caught up with the paperwork, his least favourite part of being a DCI. He hated it. Pen pushing and overseeing the troops. He would rather be out catching the villains. As he was finishing the overtime file to send it off to Wright, his mobile rang.

'Hello?'

'Well hello, DCI Watson.'

Watson sat upright. The altered voice was back.

'What the fuck do you want?'

'Tut tut, Detective Chief Inspector. I expected better from you.'

Watson got up, trying to attract Wright, Lorimer, or French's attention. To no avail.

'What's that got to do with anything?'

'Well, you and Monteith were always that creep Crompton's favourites. It's no surprise you made DCI before anyone else.'

Watson flung open Wright's door and pointed at his phone, mouthing, 'It's him.'

'Crompton didn't promote me to DCI. And he wasn't a creep,' Watson said, on edge.

'Semantics, Detective Chief Inspector. If you are considering tracing this call, I will make things easy for you and tell you where I am at this precise moment. Your wife and children look extremely lovely today, by the way. Goodbye.'

'IF YOU TOUCH MY WIFE,' Watson shouted before he realised the line was dead. 'Shit! He's after my family.' Before anyone could do anything or react, Watson bolted for the door.

'Karl, go after him,' Wright ordered. 'Go with him so he does nothing stupid. I will call for backup.'

Watson ran to his car, jumped in, and floored it. Anger and panic coursed through his body. He stopped short of hitting Lorimer. With his hands slamming on the bonnet, Lorimer stared at Watson through the windscreen.

'What the hell are you playing at?' Watson barked at Lorimer as he got in.

'Wright told me to join you. She's also ordering backup.'

'I don't need babysitting. I will kill this bastard. Threatening me is one thing, but no one threatens my family!' Watson's fist banged on the steering wheel as the car park gate slowly opened.

He dialled Sally's number through the car's system.

'Where are they?' Lorimer asked as he fastened his seat belt.

Watson gunned his car out through the gate. 'Either Sally will be picking Simon up from school, or they are at home.'

'Hello dear, this is...,' Sally's voice came through.

Watson cut her off. 'Where are you and the kids?'

'At home. Why?'

'Stay there. Don't go out or let the kids out. I won't be long.'

'Why, what's happened?' Sally's voice was full of concern.

He could hear Rachael playing in the background. A lump formed in Watson's throat.

'I'll explain when I get home, just please do as I say.' Watson cut the call short and concentrated on getting through the traffic as fast as he could.

Monteith approached Wright, who was still in her office with Costa and Underwood.

'Ma'am, I have an update. According to Amanda Ferguson, the body at Gorge Farm could be Ryan Craven's. James McGill had ordered Ryan to drive Travis Whiteman and Shaun Greatbatch to Gorge Farm last night. Ryan didn't turn up for work this morning, so Joey rang her.'

Costa and Underwood looked up. 'What's this about James McGill?'

'Thought you'd be interested,' Monteith said. 'Can uniform pick Joey up from his home? We need to know if he can corroborate Amanda's information?'

'They can pick him up from Craven Autos.'

Monteith shook his head. 'Better not. Craven Autos is across the estate from McGill's delivery business. If they notice a squad car picking up Joey, they will realise someone's talked.'

'Fair point. Ask Emma to arrange for it,' Wright said.

'Could we observe the rest of the interview?' Costa asked. 'I'm interested in finding out what this McGill is like before we raid him.'

Wright nodded. 'I don't see why not.'

Monteith walked down with Costa, Underwood, and Wright to join Sandall outside the interview room.

'DSI Wright will be observing the interview, Paul, as will DCI Costa and DI Underwood. As you know, they are interested in McGill.'

Wright signalled they would watch the video feed from the next room.

Monteith waited till they were settled and opened the door to the interview room. 'Ready?'

Both entered the interview room and sat down, Sandall starting the tapes again, as Monteith continued with the questions.

'Amanda, before our break, you said James McGill is responsible for the murders of your husband and Ryan Craven. Please, can you tell us the circumstances leading up to your husband's murder, and why you believe James McGill carried it out?'

'About a month ago, James McGill came to Craven Autos. He spoke to Ryan about having an urgent delivery waiting but none of his drivers would be back in time to take it out. So, they both asked Evan if he would like to earn some extra cash by doing the delivery.'

'Did they say what the delivery was?'

Amanda took a sip of water. 'Not that Evan said. All he was told was to get the package to an address by five o'clock. If he could get it there faster, he'd pick up a bonus on top of the extra cash McGill said he would give him.' She wavered but composed herself. 'Evan took the delivery but in his car, as there were no vans available. He was late, just missed having an accident with another car before he got there. He told me he had to slam on his brakes to avoid a collusion.' She swallowed.

Monteith allowed Amanda time to gather herself. 'What happened next?'

'He said he had arrived ten minutes late, but it wasn't just the near-miss that made him late. You see, he had put the package on the front seat, so when he slammed on the brakes, the package slid off the seat and into the footwell. It split open. He had to pull over to pick it up.' She paused again. 'He said it contained drugs.'

Monteith glanced at Sandall. Costa and Underwood must be delighted, he thought. That's the proof they were looking for.

'Did Evan tell you what type of drugs they were?'

'Some sort of tablets in bags, and a small parcel of cocaine.'

'How did Evan know it was cocaine?'

Amanda hesitated. 'Because he was a recovering drug addict. When he handed the package over, the man was furious for arriving late and for having opened the package. When Evan got back, McGill and Ryan were waiting for him. They already knew. McGill threatened to kill Evan right then, but Ryan said no. McGill then told him to watch his back and that he could close Craven Autos at any time if he wanted to.' She took a few more sips of water.

Monteith found it hard not to smile. They had got McGill on drug charges, now for the murders.

'So, Amanda. We come to the evening of Evan's disappearance. You've already given a version of what happened. Do you wish to stand by that or tell us what really happened?'

Amanda looked across anxiously at her father and the solicitor.

The solicitor took over. 'Detectives, Mrs Ferguson had described to me what she said previously. I would like to point out she was under a lot of stress then, as those we believe were responsible for her husband's murder have made threats against her. We would want assurances that she and the mechanic Joey Wells will not face prosecution for withholding information.'

Monteith was about to reply when a loud rap came on the door. He suspended the interview and went out of the room. Wright was outside. 'I can agree to that as long as she didn't commit any crime,' she said. 'Also, to let you know Joey Wells has been picked up.'

'Thank you, ma'am,' Monteith said, as he went back into the interview room.

'I've been informed that we have picked up Joey Wells and we will interview him later. It will be up to our bosses to decide what happens following that,' he explained. 'Please, Amanda, continue.'

Amanda took a deep breath. 'When Ryan told me that Evan had left the evening of his murder, he also said that a few drivers from McGill's delivery company had left shortly after.'

'Did he say what vehicle they left in?' Monteith asked with a hint of trepidation, knowing the answer could put another nail in McGill's coffin.

'I think he said it was a blue 4x4 with some weird name like Land Cruiser,' she stated and looked at her father. Highfield smiled and placed a hand on his daughter's shoulder.

'Did Ryan say which of James McGill's drivers were in the 4x4?'

Amanda nodded. 'Shaun Greatbatch, Travis Whiteman, Nicky Adams, and Curtis Jackson. He made me recite them back to him afterwards. Twice. Those names are etched into my brain.' A shiver shot through her body.

'You mentioned that both you and Ryan were threatened by McGill, the reason you didn't report Evan's disappearance till the following evening. When did that happen?'

Amanda took another sip of water before answering. 'Ryan said McGill had threatened him or if he, Joey or me went to the police, we would be next. And that we were already up to our necks in it whether or not we liked it.'

'Regarding the disappearance of Ryan Craven, what makes you and Joey think that James McGill had him killed?'

'The last time I was here, I felt terrified, paranoid even because I wanted to tell you everything. But with what McGill had said ringing in my head I couldn't. So, when I got home I rang Joey and urged him to meet me straight away.'

'What is your relationship with Joey Wells? Friends, lover?'

Amanda looked aghast at Monteith. 'Lover? Hell no. Not in a million years. I loved Evan, no one else.'

'When we arrived at your home the other week, you and Joey seemed close and you lied to us about who he was.'

'I was scared,' Amanda blurted out. 'I just said the first thing that came into my head.'

'So, why was Joey there? And why did my colleague here, Detective Constable Sandall, see you both together in town last Saturday?'

'Ryan asked Joey to keep an eye on me after Evan's murder. To try and protect me in case McGill's thugs came calling, that's all.' Amanda became agitated.

Monteith took a little pause before asking the next question. 'What happened after you asked Joey to meet you?'

'When Joey turned up, I was shocked that Ryan was with him. He hadn't told me. Ryan said he needed to see me because McGill had made another visit and Ryan was scared. McGill had ordered Ryan to drive Greatbatch and Whiteman to the farm to teach the farmer a lesson. Ryan didn't want to get involved but was terrified. After I told both Joey and Ryan what happened with our interview, we were trying to work out when to come here and tell you about everything. That's when my dad got involved.'

They all looked at Highfield, who shifted uneasily in his chair.

'How did you get roped up in all of this?' Monteith asked, his gaze not moving from the man before him.

Highfield sighed. 'When Amanda ran out of the house, I followed her because I felt she hadn't told me everything.' He smiled at his daughter. 'Now I know why. After Amanda introduced me to Joey and Ryan, they told me what had been going on and what a nasty piece of work this James McGill is. When Ryan said about what he was being forced to do, we all said he should come to you straight away. But he didn't dare. Nothing any of us said would change his mind. So, we agreed that as soon as Ryan got back, we would all come in this morning and make statements. When Joey called saying Ryan had not turned up for work, we came straight over.' Highfield took a deep breath before asking, 'Detective, do you know what happened?'

Monteith looked across the table at the three faces. 'Mr Highfield, Amanda. Last night someone set fire to Gorge Farm. When the fire was put out, a male body was found. We didn't know whose. We'll compare records of Ryan with the body.'

Screeching to a halt outside his house, Watson threw open the car door and took off towards his house, leaving Lorimer to get himself out and follow.

'SALLY!' Watson shouted, bursting through the front door.

Sally ran down the stairs to meet him. They hugged, and he held her tight.

'What's happened? You terrified me when you phoned. The children are upset because they can't go out.'

'Where are they?' Watson asked.

'Upstairs. Why?'

Behind Watson, Lorimer stood by the front door, joined by PC Gary Kendall and another uniformed officer.

Sally looked confused and on the verge of tears.

Seeing the state his boss and his wife were in, DS Lorimer led the uniformed officers outside. 'Gary, can you and your colleague go around the area and ask the neighbours if they have seen anyone acting suspiciously. And ask if they saw anyone speaking to his wife when she returned home. Also, inquire if anybody has been hanging around the kids' schools. I'll be in the house until we know the area is safe.'

When Lorimer re-entered, Watson was in the living room explaining to Sally what had happened.

'Over the last couple of weeks, I have received several phone calls. Anonymous calls and the caller has disguised their voice.'

'Why didn't you tell me before?' Sally exclaimed. 'I cannot believe you kept that from me! Have you found out who it is or what they want?'

'I'm sorry, darling. I didn't want you to panic and also didn't know whether it was a prank. So far, they haven't been on the phone long enough to trace them. The caller has always directed their ire towards me and what I stand for,' he paused, head in hands. 'Until this afternoon when he mentioned you and the kids.'

Sally looked shocked. 'What did he say?'

Watson drew a deep breath. 'Your wife and children look extremely lovely today.'

'That might explain this.' Sally showed Watson an envelope. 'It was on the doormat when I arrived home.'

Watson stared at it, then at Sally and Lorimer. On it was hand-written: "FOR DCI WATSON".

He tore open the envelope and took out the contents. Four photos of Sally and their children. On the back of each, Watson read: "Your wife and children look extremely lovely today."

CHAPTER SIXTEEN

THE AIR HAD COOLED between Watson and Sally. They tried to settle down in front of the television.

Nothing had come of the neighbourhood canvassing, and Lorimer had taken the photographs and envelope back to the station in an evidence bag to check for fingerprints. That would take time.

Watson had taken Jason and Simon aside and explained everything. He knew they were old and intelligent enough to understand, and that they would keep an eye on their little sister. He made sure they knew what to do if a stranger approached them or any of their friends.

It was family time for the rest of the evening until Rachael dropped off and had to be carried upstairs. Jason and Simon said goodnight, leaving Watson and Sally in the living room.

Sally turned off the telly and looked at her husband. 'I still don't understand. You've been receiving crank phone calls, and you have only just seen fit to tell me because of what happened today. Why didn't you tell me about the other ones? And how many were there?'

Watson squirmed. Being on the receiving end of a Sally lecture was the last thing he wanted. 'Before today, three. They were all directed at me, only me. I don't know who it is, and I didn't want to worry you.' He avoided eye contact.

'Three!' Sally exclaimed. 'When?'

'Here when you took the children school shopping. The day we found out about Kenneth, and during the BBQ when Keith and I were chatting outside.'

'The BBQ. And you didn't think to tell me or Katie!' Sally was dismayed.

'Keith wanted to go after him because he said he could smell the food, but I stopped him so as not to alarm you two and the kids.'

'Good job. You two charging through the house, off to God knows where, leaving us wondering what the hell happened.' She got up. 'Do you know who it is?'

'No, they always conceal their voice. I haven't a clue,' Watson said frustrated.

Rachael's cry broke the tension. 'Mum! I can't sleep.'

'I'll be up,' Sally answered. Before she went up, she said, 'While I'm upstairs, make another drink for us and while you do that, think carefully, very carefully, about those calls. What did they say? How did they say it? It may not have stood out before, but now, after those creepy photos. He *knows* you.'

<hr>

The clock on the wall read 9.12 p.m. and everyone in the office was tired. Monteith and Sandall had interviewed Joey Wells after he had requested a solicitor and the on-call solicitor had arrived. Not only had he corroborated everything, he also told them that McGill was trying to force Ryan to put packages of drugs in clients' cars when they brought them in for customising, by hiding them behind false panels in the car's interior and bodywork. Ryan had held fast refusing McGill, but the pressure had been building.

French had updated them on the registration numbers from the dashcam footage. The Toyota Land Cruiser had been bought at a second-hand auction two weeks before by one Trevor White. The Mercedes was registered to James McGill.

They had agreed that Highfield should take Amanda up to Lincoln for her safety until everything with McGill had been sorted. Nobody wanted a repeat of what had transpired at Gorge Farm.

Joey refused to take time off. 'Someone has to look after Ryan's business,' he replied. 'McGill may have invested money into the business, but it is still Ryan's name over the door.'

Wright ordered Montcith, Sandall, and French to call it a night and go home, which they didn't hesitate to do.

She settled down with Costa and Underwood. It was time to work on a plan to take down James McGill.

The taxi reached the Thelwell Estate. In the rear, a heavily intoxicated Davy Clayton. After spending most of the afternoon in court, he was out on bail. He spent the rest of the afternoon and evening getting drunk and aggressive, wanting to fight anyone who dared. By the time he had found a taxi to take him home, he'd been thrown out of four pubs and one club. Even his friends had gradually disappeared as the evening went on.

Stopping at a junction, a group of men surrounded the taxi. The rear door opened with a bang and Davy was dragged out onto the road. They paid off the driver, who rapidly beat a hasty retreat.

Three of the men manhandled a cursing and swearing Davy. They held him up in front of Freddie Anderson. Davy stopped and stared straight at him, trying to head-butt him but failing miserably. Freddie's right-handed punch landed on Davy's cheek, followed by another to the solar plexus. Davy gasped for breath as he threw up the evening's beer and kebab on the feet of the guys holding him.

Freddie laughed. He signalled,said, and his brothers threw Davy into the back of a transit. He joined his brothers in the front. 'That was fun.' Freddie grinned as Andrew started the engine.

Ten minutes later, Andrew directed the transit in through the doors and parked up in the middle of the warehouse. Freddie and Luke jumped out and helped to drag Davy out of the back. They tied him to a cement-covered steel post, supporting the roof. A mumbling Davy, with an already swollen left eye, slumped against his restraints.

Woody Anderson stepped out of his car, smoothed down his coat, and strode towards them. As he reached Davy, he grabbed his hair and pulled his head up, studying the mess Freddie had made.

'Not so brave now, are you?' Woody whispered in Davy's ear. He broke out laughing.

'Fuck off,' Davy slurred.

Woody stopped mid-laugh and nodded at Freddie, who landed two more punches on Davy's body.

Davy bent double, howling in pain.

'Do I have your attention?' Woody said.

Davy grunted.

'I thought after our previous discussions I made it clear that you and your brother should leave and let the big boys run things.' Spreading his arms, Woody continued, 'But oh no, what do you do? You burn down one of my garages. And you still go about your business as if nothing has happened. We warned you, and you didn't pay heed; now recompense for losses incurred is in order.' He nodded again to Freddie.

His son stepped forward and aimed a flurry of punches at Davy's head and body. Davy tried to struggle free. Without success.

Woody moved forward again, taking a pouch from his inside jacket pocket. Opening the pouch, he took out a syringe. He put the needle into Davy's arm and emptied the contents.

'Dump him somewhere on the outskirts.'

'Yes, Dad,' Andrew and Luke said.

They cut Davy's body loose and dragged him back to the van.

'Assume it will work?' Freddie asked.

Woody put the pouch back in his jacket and smiled. 'It's time to finish this... permanently.'

Wednesday

Joey opened up the shutters on the front of Craven Autos. After he'd got back home from being interviewed last night, he'd rang Amanda. She had told him she was going to stay with her parents in Lincoln, pleading for him to get away until McGill was caught. Again, he had refused.

Joey checked the diary to see if they could postpone any of the cars coming in for modifications, followed by what was required to finish on the ones they had in. One by one, the other mechanics arrived, surprised that Ryan was still not in. Joey gathered them together and revealed that Ryan was missing, possibly dead, and that Evan had been murdered. He was careful not to mention McGill - if he had, they would have charged over and taken on McGill. He wouldn't have blamed them - he had lost count of the number of times he had the same thoughts.

The office phone rang. It was Detective Monteith. Joey slumped back into the chair as Monteith confirmed that Ryan's body was found in the burned-out farmhouse. His skull had been caved in before the fire, so it was also being treated as murder.

Joey promised they wouldn't take things into their own hands.

Joey relayed the information to everybody and suggested only working on existing orders and not taking on any new customers for the week.

In her office, Wright said to Watson and Lorimer, 'I'm worried. After four phone calls, this crank caller posted photos of Sally and your children. What the hell do they want? What is their motive?'

'If I knew that, I would have had my hands around his neck before now,' Watson said, frustrated. 'I went over the calls with Sally last night. Something's nagging me. I think I know who it is. Just can't put my finger on it.' He related the contents of all four calls to his colleagues.

'You understand why I thought it was a prank first? It's obvious it is much more now, but what?' he exclaimed.

Wright turned to Lorimer. 'What about the photos? Any finger-prints?'

'I'm still waiting for forensics,' Lorimer said.

'Terry,' Wright said, 'Could it be someone you used to work with?'

Watson frowned. 'That narrows it down to a few hundred. Not really helping.' He thought. 'I probably pissed off many people in those six years inside and outside the force, but to this extent?'

'Sorry, but I just had a call from Billy Clayton,' Monteith said, standing in the door opening. 'Davy's in hospital, found in a back alley on the outskirts of Thelwell. Beaten and drugged up. Billy's on the warpath and pointing the finger at the Andersons.'

———

Andrew pulled the car in front of the Anderson family home. His father stood waiting. Luke and Freddie followed in the Transit. Woody sauntered to the car and looked at Freddie. Freddie put his thumb up, Woody opened the door and slipped into the passenger seat.

'Ready, Dad?'

Woody nodded. 'Ready.'

Both vehicles moved off, the occupants oblivious that their every step was being observed.

———

The drug unit had been observing McGill and his team and had gathered lots of evidence of shipments, deliveries, and which routes were taken. They'd set up office in another unit, the owner of which was only too happy to help, having had multiple run-ins with McGill.

The information Amanda Ferguson and Joey Wells had provided was the icing on the cake and just what DCI Costa and DI Underwood needed to organise the take down of McGill's empire in London, Cambridge, and Ravenswood.

Watson and Monteith parked up and went into the A&E of Ravenswood hospital looking for Davy. The receptionist asked them to wait while she checked it.

'I hate hospitals.' Monteith shuddered.

'Is that after spending time in here when the Russells took you?' Watson asked.

'Among other things. Visiting Mac's morgue doesn't help. That place gives me the creeps.'

Watson laughed. 'Mac's visitors will not rise like the walking dead.'

'I wouldn't be surprised if they did. The way Mac talks to them, it's a wonder they don't answer.'

'According to Mac, they do,' Watson laughed.

The waiting room door opened and in came Billy Clayton, looking like a ghost.

'How is he?' Watson asked.

Billy stuck a plastic cup under the water cooler in the corner and watched it fill. 'Not great,' he replied as he sat down on one of the well-worn chairs. 'He was drunk, badly beaten, and the paramedics found a needle mark on his arm. They are hoping to move him to a ward soon. Waiting for a bed.'

'I didn't think Davy used drugs?' Monteith said, sitting down next to Billy.

'He's started after Dad died. Ecstasy, the odd bit of coke according to his friends I have spoken to. But never, ever did he inject. Scared of needles. Hates going to the dentist in case he needs a filling.' Billy knocked back the cup of water in one, throwing the cup at the bin and missing.

'What makes you think it was Woody Anderson?' Monteith asked.

Billy picked the cup up and put it into the bin. 'A friend saw Davy being dumped out of the back of Anderson's Ford Transit on the outskirts of the estate. He caught a glimpse of Andrew behind the wheel as they hurried away. Word got back to me quickly after and I came down here straight away.'

'Is your friend sure it was Andrew Anderson?'

'Course he is,' Billy snapped. 'You think he made it up?'

'No. No, Billy, I didn't mean it that way. We need to make certain of all the facts before...'

'Before what? You deal with the Andersons?' Billy shouted, getting up. 'Davy said you weren't going to do anything. And he was right. What *have* you done?'

'We'll follow it up. Just don't get your own back, for Davy's sake.'

'I'm going nowhere while Davy's in here.'

'Good. Leave it to us.'

Billy headed for the door. Opening it, he looked over his shoulder. '*I* won't do anything. As for the rest of the estate, well, I can't speak for them.'

He was gone before they realised what he'd said.

Monteith looked at Watson. 'SHIT.'

—

The ambush on the Andersons had been carefully organised and would have taken place even before Davy was beaten and drugged up. Plans had been made at the meeting in the Royal Oak. The families who'd previously supported the Claytons were fed up with Woody and his sons. When Woody Anderson had revealed his intent for the estate, that was the final straw. Davy's beating just added to the anger of the blood-thirsty mob.

As the Andersons made their way through their part of the estate, passing the homes of families that had switched to their side, small groups of men clustered by the road and at the end of alleyways, watching as they went by. Once the car and van had passed, the road behind was blocked off by cars and other obstacles. As they rounded the bend before the turn-off leading into the city centre, another barrier blocked that road. Further along the main road was a heavy barrier. Twenty men across the road in front of them blocked any progress. All were armed.

There was no escape. The cars came to a screeching stop. Tyre smoke billowed out.

In the car, Woody and Andrew stared at the horde in front of them. Behind the wheel of the Transit, Freddie tried to reverse, but only got a couple of yards. Barriers and another group of men were preventing any movement.

'What's going on?' a voice from the back of the Transit shouted.

'Stay still and wait,' Luke shouted back. 'We have a problem. The bastards knew we were coming.'

Bricks and lumps of concrete rained down on the car and Transit. Andrew opened his door, trying to make a run for it.

'GET US OUT OF HERE,' Woody bellowed.

Andrew stared at his dad, shut the door, and slammed his foot on the accelerator.

'I'm taking out as many as I can, Dad,' he said grimly.

'Go for it.'

Through the shattered window screen, Andrew drove straight into the crowd in front of them.

He didn't get far. After striking the first few, sending them over the bonnet, the car came to a shuddering halt as it crashed into the side of another car placed across the road.

Luke and Freddie watched in horror from the Transit. Freddie revved the engine and tried to swing the van around. He failed miserably, and crashed through a low front garden wall.

The mob soon enveloped them. One attacker opened the driver's door and Freddie kicked him in the face with his boot, sending the man stumbling backward, blood streaming from his nose.

Freddie kicked out at anyone close to the door until the attackers got hold of his ankle. An iron bar came down with full force and shattered his leg. Freddie's shrieks of pain rang out as they dragged him out of the Transit. Punches, boots, and cricket bats rained down on Freddie.

Luke had also been dragged out of the Transit. He was up against its side, fighting off anyone who moved within reach. A brick hit Luke on the side of the head, and he crumpled onto the ground.

The back doors of the Transit flew open and the six balaclava-wearing gang broke out, waving baseball bats at everyone around them. It didn't take long for them to be overpowered.

Andrew and Woody were battling hard to go on in their car. Andrew slammed it into reverse, but the engine didn't start. Both were now panicking, grabbing hold of whatever they could. The mob cheered and wrenched the doors away, grabbing at father and son. Others reached through the shattered glass and directed blows at what body parts they could reach. Woody and Andrew didn't stand a chance; they were hauled out of the car.

The beating began.

CHAPTER SEVENTEEN

WATSON AND MONTEITH HAD been too late.

They watched the ambulances come in back from the Thelwell Estate. Watson had spoken to the A&E duty manager, asking him to let them know if any of the Andersons had been brought in.

'I find it hard to believe you knew nothing about what went on,' Monteith said to Billy. 'Not after what you said before you disappeared earlier.'

Billy grinned. 'How could I? I've been here all night with Davy. Besides, a wise man once told me, "One thing you need to learn in business, legal or illegal, don't show up without a backup plan".'

'Your dad was a wise man.'

'Wasn't my dad but Woody Anderson, during a meeting.' He paused. 'In fact, we had a meeting of our own on our side of the estate. We planted spies with the Andersons, making them believe some families had switched sides. It worked,' he stated. 'The assault on Davy was just the oil on the fire. Oh, and don't think you can pin any of this on me or my brother. We were left out of the attack plan. Me being here all night with Davy came in handy.' He grinned again. 'The perfect alibi.'

A doctor called Watson over, informing him that Woody Anderson and his sons had been admitted to A&E.

'You stay here,' Watson ordered Billy.

'Don't worry, I'm not going anywhere near them. Though it would be good to see the state they're in.'

James McGill watched the mechanics leaving Craven Autos.

'Where the hell are they going, Travis?'

Both men were standing outside the Wild West Unit after seeing off the last of the delivery vans.

'Looks like the news of Ryan's demise has filtered through,' Whiteman chuckled. 'With your money propping up Craven Autos, what are you planning to do with it now?'

'Take over. What else do you expect? Let them have a few days to sort things out, and I will present a rescue package to buy the business outright.'

'Before you concentrate on that, let me remind you we have bigger things to worry about this week. That large shipment is expected on Friday and if we don't get the deliveries right, it will be *this* business that'll be taken over.'

'How can I forget?' McGill huffed, walking back to his office. 'The powers that be have made that clear on more than one occasion.'

From inside Craven Autos, Joey observed the men, hands balled into fists. Part of him wanted to walk straight over and attack the pair of them. Murderers, they were.

DI Monteith's words of warning rang loud in his head. *Stay away from McGill.* Easy to say, he thought, but who's going to tell McGill to stay away from Craven Autos?

Two squad cars parked up close to the hospital's doors, ready to take assailants who were fit enough to the station. Kendall and Dixon, with four uniformed officers, joined Watson and Monteith in the reception area.

'The doctors will release Woody Anderson and one of his sons, Andrew, soon,' Watson informed them. 'I want them in custody at headquarters as soon as.' He paused. 'As to Luke and Freddie, they weren't so lucky. Freddie's leg was shattered and needs operating on. Luke is in worse shape even. He's been put in an induced coma and rushed to the operating theatre after scans of the brain showed a swelling and a possible internal bleed. You and you,' Watson pointed at two uniformed officers, 'will escort Freddie and Luke to the operating theatres. Freddie has already been cautioned. You will stay with them until they are released.'

The two officers nodded and went off.

'You two,' Watson addressed the other two uniformed bodies, 'will keep guard of Woody and Andrew, as they have been violent against the staff already. Don't keep them out of your sight until they've been locked up at headquarters.'

A little boy approached them and tugged at Kendall's trousers. Kendall knelt. 'And what's your name?'

'Michael,' the boy whispered.

His mother joined them. 'He loves the police,' she explained. 'He has a load of toy police cars, and he dresses up as a policeman when he plays with them.'

Kendall showed his peaked cap and placed it on Michael's head. The boy's face lit up as he looked up at his mother.

They all smiled. Watson made a mental note. So often, the police were accused of being not visible, he thought. Kendall had just made a small dent in that by making the boy's day in front of a crowded waiting room.

Billy wandered in. 'Davy's asleep, so I thought I would stretch my legs.'

'Have you told him what happened?' Monteith asked.

'Oh yes. He wants to punch their lights out. Took me and two nurses to cool him down,' Billy laughed.

A uniformed officer approached Watson and signalled they were ready to discharge Woody and Andrew.

'You had better make yourself scarce,' Watson told Billy, but it was too late. Both Woody and Andrew, handcuffed, appeared.

'BILLY CLAYTON. YOU BASTARD.' Woody's voice boomed as he struggled to free himself from the restraint of the officer.

Billy grinned and stepped towards the front door.

At that same moment, Woody freed himself and ran towards Billy. 'I'm going to kill you, Clayton.'

He didn't notice Kendall, who was still on his knees and now stuck out his leg. Woody flew onto the floor at the feet of Watson and Monteith.

Kendall and Dixon grabbed Woody and dragged him up.

'Get him out of here,' Monteith said.

Kendall and Dixon took Woody to one of the waiting cars. Two other officers did the same with Andrew.

'The interviews should be entertaining,' Watson remarked. He felt a tug on his trousers. Looking down, he saw the little lad Kendall had been talking to. In his hand was Kendall's cap.

Watson knelt and smiled. 'Thank you. I'll make sure PC Kendall gets it back,' he said, watching the lad run back to his mother.

When Watson and Monteith arrived back at the office, Matthews was raging.

'What the hell went on? Why did we not have sight of what was going on there? For fuck's sake, we should've stopped it before it had even started.' He looked at Watson. 'I want facts. NOW.'

'I'll give you the facts, sir,' Watson said calmly, trying to diffuse the situation. Getting into a slanging match with Matthews would not help things. This was time for composure. He took a deep breath and informed Matthews.

Matthews bristled. 'I still haven't heard why we didn't prevent this slaughter from happening.'

Watson looked at Wright, who took over. 'I'm sorry, sir, but we have kept you constantly updated about the situation on the Thelwell Estate. We warned it might explode. We just didn't know when. And we cannot be everywhere at the same time. We do not have the manpower. She paused. 'Sir, may I suggest we continue this in my office? DCI Watson, will you join us?'

Without saying a single word, Matthews strode straight towards Wright's office.

Watson turned to Monteith and Lorimer. 'We have some guests downstairs that will need to be interviewed soon. Can you two sort that out please?' He followed Wright and Matthew and pushed the door shut behind him. He realised this was going to be a strained muscle-flexing meeting. Battle lines were going to be drawn, and God help anyone who crossed them.

'Sir, I don't appreciate shouting in the office, in front of everyone like that. Coming down here and having a go at my staff. I trust and back them with my life. They work hard to make Ravenswood a safer place. If you have any trouble with anyone in my department, you can have my warrant card now.' Wright yanked open a drawer in her desk, reached in, and placed her warrant card on the desk.

'You can add mine to that,' Watson added as he placed his down next to Wright's.

Matthews looked flustered. 'You make a fair point. Take your cards back, both of you.'

'You put me in charge of this department, to run as I see fit,' Wright said, sticking her warrant card back. 'DCI Watson and DI Monteith have been keeping a close eye on the estate. Talking to residents, especially the Claytons. Frequently, we have pointed out that something was going to happen.'

Watson added, 'You mentioned you were looking to sort out the estate. With Woody and Andrew Anderson in the cells downstairs and Freddie and Luke in hospital, this is our chance to clear out the estate.'

Matthews nodded. 'I see. Where are Billy and Davy Clayton? If we hit the estate, we don't want to be seen cleaning out only one side.'

'Billy is still with Davy in hospital. I understand they are looking to release Davy later this afternoon or tomorrow.'

Matthews stood and wandered over to the window looking out on the city centre.

'I want a waterproof plan,' Matthews said, turning back. 'How the raid will work, what places and areas are going to be hit. Also, what manpower you require.' He looked at his watch. 'It's a quarter past three now. I need it on my desk first thing tomorrow.'

He walked towards the door and opened it. 'One last thing. Next time either of you pulls a stunt like that with the warrant card, I will take it off you. You two may be in charge of this department, but let me remind you, you still answer to me.' And he was gone.

'That went better than I expected,' Wright said as she stood to go out of her office to address the team about the raid.

'What gets me, ma'am,' said Watson. 'We told Matthews repeatedly about the estate. And it's now when we have the drug unit raid against James McGill on Friday, together with interviewing the Andersons, the Claytons, and whoever else over the riot that he decides he needs a strategy for raiding the estate. Something's got to give, surely.'

'If we release the Andersons on caution, they will go after Billy and Davy,' French added. 'Couldn't we get the drug unit to suspend their raid?'

Wright shook her head. 'Not a chance. Their operation will coincide with other connected raids across the Southeast and London. We can't get out of it.'

Watson was frustrated. 'When are we going to know their plan? We have heard nothing so far from Underwood and Costa. They wanted our help, but have they asked for it?'

'No doubt they will when we are raiding Thelwell,' Sandall said dismissively.

Others nodded in agreement.

'So inter-unit co-operation takes place before the stuff we have been working on?' asked Watson.

Wright responded. 'I know what you are saying, but just take a minute. We will get rid of James McGill. Finally.'

Watson glanced at Wright. 'We want McGill for the murders of Evan Ferguson and Ryan Craven. They only want him for drug distribution. Who gets him?'

'I'll leave that to Matthews and Costa,' Wright answered. But I'll argue that we should get the first crack as we are talking about murder.'

'Absolutely,' Watson agreed. 'If Costa and Underwood get their way, who's going to tell Amanda Ferguson that we are handing over McGill, Greatbatch, and the others not knowing if they will face trial over Evan's murder? We need to know their plan.'

Wright nodded. 'I will speak to Matthews. With the drugs raid set for Friday morning, we will need to act fast.'

'We have the intelligence to bring him down,' Watson reminded Wright. 'All we need is the go-ahead.'

'Why don't we just arrest the bastard?' Sandall asked.

'Because we need to play this by the book. If Matthews gives us the go-ahead, then it's down to him to smooth it over with Costa and Underwood. As I said, I will see him later,' Wright stated. 'Now, let's focus on Woody and Andrew Anderson, who are enjoying our hospitality. Their solicitor must be here by now. Have we got all the facts ready and correct?'

Sandall answered, 'Their lawyer has been here for the last half an hour. Arrived when you were in your office. DI Monteith and DS Lorimer will start the interviews soon.'

'And Billy told us the build-up to the attack,' Watson added. 'We need to bring Billy and Davy in after we have dealt with the Andersons. They have some explaining of their own to do. The boss will want everybody on that estate dealt with.' He added, 'Sandall and French, can you collate all the information we have about the Thelwell Estate? Where have we raided before and what transpired? Is there any CCTV footage of any part of what went on there this morning or the lead-up to it?'

***

'I would like it put on record that you have held my clients against their will for over two hours,' the solicitor stated as soon as Monteith and Lorimer entered the interview room.

'Did you hear anything, DS Lorimer?' Monteith asked as he laid his file down on the table.

'Only a rush of hot air,' Lorimer replied. Someone must have left a window open.'

Monteith finished setting his things down on the table and looked up. 'Afternoon, Mr Anderson, and Mr Taylor-Brown.'

Taylor-Brown straightened his tie. 'I said my clients have been...'

'We heard you, Mr Taylor-Brown.'

The solicitor was about to protest, but Woody put a hand on his arm. 'Don't take the bait, Charles. They're only trying to wind you up.'

'Now, Mr Edward Anderson,' Monteith started.

'Woody, please. Mr Edward Anderson sounds too polite.'

Monteith stared at Woody. '*Mr Anderson,*' he emphasised. 'This morning you were involved in an altercation with several people on the Thelwell Estate.'

'An altercation? Is that what you call it?' Woody's eyes flashed with anger.

'What would you call it, Mr Anderson?' Monteith looked straight at him.

'They attacked us. We were ambushed by thugs connected to that Clayton lot. You should do something about that family. Look at the CCTV footage; you should be able to find out who attacked us,' Woody spat out.

'We are doing so, though they are regularly broken,' Monteith stated.

'I suppose you're going to charge me for that as well.' Woody got out of his chair, pacing around the room.

'Sit down, Mr Anderson. Now.' Monteith ordered.

The solicitor said, 'My client apologises for the outburst. He's stressed and worried after the attack on him and his family. As you know, two of his sons are still in the hospital. He would like to help you with your inquiries, and look after his sons as soon as possible.'

Woody Anderson nodded.

'Thank you,' Monteith replied. 'Now, let's continue this interview. Can you explain to us what happened this morning leading up to the attack?'

'My sons and I were leaving the estate going into town, Andrew with me in the car. Luke and Freddie followed in our van.'

'And there was no one else in either vehicle?'

'No,' Woody said, getting tetchy.

'When we got to the main road, it was blocked,' Woody stated. 'They blocked every side street off with barriers and people. We had nowhere to go. I saw Freddie trying to reverse the van, but they stopped him.'

'What did you do next?' Monteith asked.

'We feared for our lives. I told Andrew to get us out of there. He floored it and drove at the people in front of us on the road.'

'Did they get out of the way? Did you hit any?'

'Detective,' Taylor-Brown interjected. 'What type of question is that? You heard my client say he feared for his life. He just wanted to get out of there.'

'I understand. You couldn't turn round because they were blocking the road and, as you've said, Freddie tried that and failed.'

Woody shook his head, anger in his voice. 'They had put two cars across the road, and we hit them. They surrounded us, couldn't get out of the car. Then the missiles came raining down. Bricks, concrete. Smashed all the windows. They ripped the doors open and dragged out us. Animals, the lot of them,' he spat. 'Baying for our blood. And they would have got it if you lot hadn't turned up.'

'Thank you,' Monteith said. 'We are going to suspend the interview for an hour now. Mr Anderson, I want you to use this hour wisely. Whatever your beef is with the Claytons, it has gone out of control and needs to stop now. We will bring to justice whoever attacked you, but you need to help us.'

'And what about the Claytons? Will you be saying the same to them?'

'You leave the Claytons alone. We will speak to them.'

———

Wright and Watson stood watching in the video room next door.

'Do we have anything concrete to hold them on?' Wright asked.

'The attack on Davy? But it's flimsy until we interview Davy. Do you want me to bring Billy and him in after he's released from the hospital?'

Wright looked at Watson. 'Will he listen to you?'

Watson rubbed his face with both hands and let out a sigh. 'If I can talk to Billy first, maybe, just maybe, he will see sense.'

CHAPTER EIGHTEEN

'GET OFF, LET ME OUT,' Davy shouted at Billy as they walked through their front door. 'I want to get my hands on that bastard,' he bristled, shoving his brother.

Billy sent Davy tumbling backwards onto the sofa. 'Listen to yourself. You've just been discharged from hospital, and you want to tackle the Andersons. You! A one-man army.'

Davy tried to get back to his feet, only for Billy to push him back down. 'Didn't you see all that when we came in?' Billy pointed out of the front window.

'That out there is courtesy of our friends. Our friends on this side of the estate. Friends who have backed us, friends who have risen and stood by us since Dad died. None of them want the Andersons around. They want rid of them as much as we do. While I was making sure you were alright, our friends took on the Andersons. I didn't ask them, and they made certain we weren't around when it all kicked off.'

'I still want my crack at them,' Davy grumbled.

'And you will, dear brother, just not now. Woody and Andrew are in police custody, Freddie, and Luke are in hospital. I spoke to Mr Watson and Mr Monteith there. Freddie and Luke are in a bad way.'

Davy laughed. 'Good. About time.'

Billy sat down. 'They also said they will need to talk to us.'

'About what?'

'What happened this morning. And regarding who gave you the drugs and beating. We can get the Andersons on that; someone saw you being dumped from the back of their van last night. All you need to do is remember what happened before. I'll tell you what,' Billy continued, his tone quieter. 'Relax this evening, we will go over everything together tomorrow. Then we will speak to Mr Watson and Mr Monteith. I'll give them a ring now to say this, so they don't send anyone tonight. I will say that you are not in a fit state to be questioned today and you shouldn't have been discharged. Hopefully, that will placate the situation.'

Davy nodded. 'Okay, point taken.'

***

French knocked on DCI Wright's door.

'Come in Emma, don't stand on ceremony,' Wright said. She was behind her desk, with Watson sitting in front of her.

'Paul and I have run through the database and found some material on previous raids on the Thelwell Estate, but nothing worth mentioning. We have ended up empty-handed.'

'Doesn't surprise me,' Watson commented. 'As soon as they get wind we are coming, everything disappears. They look after their own,' he added. 'Woody and his sons discovered that this morning. Tried to take over the estate, and the estate fought back.'

'The boss will nevertheless want to raid,' Wright stated. 'They might look after their own, but we look after the whole of Ravenswood and that includes the Thelwell Estate.'

James McGill cruised his Mercedes in the outside lane of the parkway, fingers tapping away on the steering wheel to the music on the local radio. His concentration was broken by his phone ringing in its cradle.

'McGill,' he announced, using the car's hands-free system.

A harsh cockney male voice entered through the car's speakers. 'You all set for the shipment on Friday?'

'Yes, boss, all good.'

It had better be. After that last cock up, we will be watching this time.'

McGill felt a cold, icy chill envelop his body.

'Are you there, McGill?' the voice rasped.

'Yes, yes. Sorry needed to change lanes,' McGill replied tersely.

'If we hear you have not made all the deliveries, we will collect payment from *you*...'

McGill stared ahead as the call ended. A threat he knew would be carried through. Too late to pull out. He was up to his neck in it.

They moved the action meeting late in the afternoon to Superintendent Matthews' larger one. Decisions and a timeframe had to be worked out.

'How did the interview go?' Matthews asked Watson.

'Okay, sir, suspended for now. Anderson's sons are still in hospital. Luke has only a fifty-fifty chance of recovery. The next twenty-four hours will be critical, so we have released Woody and Andrew on police bail with strict conditions. Reporting to the police station once a day and forbidden to go anywhere close to the Claytons' house or the surrounding roads. And I've had a call from Billy Clayton who will bring in Davy for questioning tomorrow morning.'

Matthews nodded. 'Good, good.'

Watson continued, 'We are still gathering witness statements. We have caught and bailed thirty residents from the estate. Some witnesses have refused to make a statement. Oh, and when we interviewed Woody, he failed to mention the six masked men in the back of their van.' He smirked.

Wright took over. 'Sir, with your permission, we wanted to discuss the drugs raid on McGill set for Friday.'

'Yes.' Matthews sat up straighter, his voice full of importance now. 'I've had DCI Costa and DI Underwood in here today, completing the details. DCI Watson will lead the team from our area, supported by DI Monteith and DS Lorimer. It will be an early morning raid.'

Wright scrunched up her face. 'And when were you going to tell me that my detectives were to be a part of this raid? Costa and Underwood have been here all week, and this is the first time we get details.'

'I'm telling you now, DSI Wright,' Matthews replied with a steely voice.

Watson could hear Wright's sharp intake of breath. *Here it comes.* He suppressed a smile.

'I take it DCI Costa will be in charge?' Wright asked.

'Yes, why?'

Wright's voice was measured. 'Why does it require two DCIs?'

'I want DCI Watson at the location, and I will tell you why,' Matthews said. 'I don't trust Costa and Underwood. I've heard they have a habit of cutting corners. We require someone down there to make certain they run this appropriately.'

'Who's going to stick the cuffs on James McGill and the rest?' Watson asked. 'I assume Costa is going to demand to take charge of that as well. Will he give over McGill to us without a fight?'

Matthews beamed. 'McGill and his henchmen are ours. Murder and attempted murder trumps a drug bust every time. Costa can have all the drugs and whoever they deliver to. It's no skin off my nose. McGill stays here.'

Sandall trudged up the stairs to his flat, cursing. Why hadn't they repaired the lift yet? After another late finish, all he wanted was a hot shower, a quick ready meal in the microwave, a beer, and crashing on the sofa in front of the telly.

Glancing at the front door across the landing, he realised he hadn't seen his new neighbour, Caroline, and her sister Jordan since they moved in. Opening his door, he could hear laughing coming from their flat. Sounds like they have settled in. Tonight, he didn't feel like being neighbourly. Perhaps over the weekend?

Thursday

'Dad, are you coming on Saturday?' Simon sat at the kitchen table, picking at his breakfast. Saturday was Simon's first big game for the Ravenswood Under Fifteens. He had been training with them for the last month since being spotted by their scout playing for Ryland's Under Fourteens last season.

'I will do my best,' said Terry as he washed up his breakfast things. 'It depends on what's on at work. We are incredibly busy at the minute, though.'

'It's a tremendous occasion for Simon,' Sally said softly as she placed her breakfast items in the sink.

'I realise that, but we are up to our neck in it,' Terry replied as he picked up a tea towel. 'Hopefully, we can get everything sorted by Saturday. If not, I will ask the boss for the morning off.'

Katie took Terry's hands in hers. 'The doctor told you to take it easy. Thought you would be more desk-bound. They have rushed you off your feet since day one. I'm concerned about you.'

'Try convincing the scum bags of Ravenswood! They're the ones doing it.' Terry planted some washing up liquid bubbles on her nose and walked off.

Sally raised her voice. 'I'm not finished with you, Detective Chief Inspector Watson. We'll continue this later.'

Katie perched on the edge of the bath, looking down at her hands. Keith stuck his head around the door. 'I'm off shortly. Rebecca is getting Pixie ready for school.' He looked at his wife. 'You alright, love?'

Katie glanced up, wiping tears from her eyes. 'I'm pregnant.' She handed him the Clearblue stick.

'Bloody hell. How long gone?'

Katie stood up, snatched some toilet paper, and blew her nose. 'Two months. Spain.'

Keith grinned. 'That was a great holiday. Sea, sangria, and now a baby. Why the tears?'

'I'm too old to have another baby!'

Keith took her in his arms. 'Shush. No, you're not.'

'Why's mummy crying?' Rebecca and Pixie were standing by the door.

Katie removed her tears and looked at Keith. 'Will you or shall I?'

Keith smiled. 'After you, mama.'

Katie giggled. 'Girls, I'm going to have a baby! You're going to have a baby brother or sister.'

The girls squealed in delight and joined the family hug. It had been too long since the family had been this close, Keith realised. Mainly due to him. Hopefully, things were turning out for the better.

'Right girls, school. Get your things ready,' Keith broke the reverie.

'Can I choose the baby's name?' asked Pixie, jumping up and down.

'You can help, yes,' Katie said. 'But that's a long way off still. Now, get your things and go.'

After they had gone, Katie turned back to Keith. 'I wonder what names she will come up with.'

'The mind boggles,' Keith laughed. 'I fancy either Miguel or Sierra.'

Katie playfully slapped his arm. 'You would.'

'When are you going to tell the dragon?'

'Don't remind me. The later the better.'

—

Billy and Davy Clayton arrived at the police headquarters short-ly after eleven o'clock. Watson and Monteith lead them through to an interview room. They could see Davy was on edge, pacing around. They managed to calm him down and get him in his seat for the interview.

The interview started with Billy relating the deteriorating relationship with the Andersons, from the first meeting at the Carpenters Arms to the one at the Dragon's Den car park and Billy's broken nose.

Monteith said, 'Thanks for that, Billy. Now, Davy, you are still on bail regarding the arson attack on Anderson's garage.'

'I didn't do it,' Davy shouted, thumping his fists on the table. 'I didn't do it. You *have* to believe me.'

Billy tried to calm his brother down. 'We thought about doing something. We considered taking a garage out, even scouted the surrounding area, but realised it would be too dangerous.'

'You went to the Anderson's side of the estate?'

'You sound surprised. Thanks to Dad, we know everything about the Andersons, where their businesses are and how they are run.'

'Your dad taught you well, Billy,' Monteith acknowledged. 'So, do you know who did it? It's still an ongoing investigation.'

'Talk is it's either a disgruntled customer or one of their own. Goes by the name of Speedy.' Davy looked at the detectives. 'I know who it is. I saw Speedy.'

They all stared at him.

'What? Speedy?' Billy exclaimed.

'Yep. I saw Speedy set fire to the garage. I was going to do it, set fire to the garage. Speedy beat me to it. It was already alight. Saw him climb over the fence onto the sports field, then come back as if he had only just got there.'

'Do you know Speedy's name?' Watson asked.

Billy responded. 'Steven Rivers. Lives at the far end of the estate.'

Watson and Monteith exchanged glances. This was going better than they'd thought.

He proceeded. 'Davy, can we take you back a couple of nights ago? Can you recall anything from before you ended up in the hospital?'

Davy rocked his head and rubbed his left arm. He stopped and peered down to a spot on the inside of his lower arm just below the elbow. A small pinprick was just about visible. 'Somebody put something in me,' he mumbled. Further down his arm were marks around the wrist. He studied his other wrist. 'I... they tied me up.'

Billy stared concerned at his brother. 'Can we take a break, Mr Watson?'

'Just a minute, Billy. Davy, can you remember who tied you up?' Watson pressed.

Davy lifted his head, fixing on a spot on the wall behind the detectives. He started shaking, closing his eyes, hands on head.

'Mr Watson, please,' Billy plead.

Watson nodded. 'We'll give you fifteen minutes. A police officer is outside if you require anything.'

He walked out of the interview room. Monteith followed. 'This is going to be tougher than we expected,' Monteith exclaimed as they got into the lift back to the office. 'Davy's done a complete one-eighty.'

As they entered the office, Lorimer asked, 'How's the statement going? Davy playing silly buggers?'

'Slow and no. The run-in with the Andersons has hammered the wind out of his sails.'

'Have they given us anything?' French asked.

Yes. Emma, check our records for Steven Rivers aka Speedy. He is an Anderson man but Davy spotted him around the Anderson garage when it went up in flames. Put the finger on him starting it.'

'Will do.' French turned back to her computer.

'Bloody hell, he must have a death wish, this Rivers fellow,' Lorimer commented.

'Yes,' Watson agreed. 'He better have made himself scarce or he could be the next one in hospital.'

'Boss, while you're here,' Sandall said, picking up a file and making his way across to Watson. 'I think you might find this interesting.'

'I'll hold you to that,' Watson joked, taking the file. 'What are you going to do if I don't find it interesting?'

'Make him listen to Pink Floyd continuously for a day,' Monteith shouted from the coffee area.

'That's a good idea,' Watson agreed. 'Paul, you up for the challenge?'

'Challenge accepted, boss,' he grinned. 'Remember those photos you sent for fingerprinting?'

Watson's blood ran cold. 'He's in the system?'

'Not exactly.'

Watson looked curiously at him and then opened the file. He blanched as he read the contents. Then read it again. 'Thanks, Paul,' he said as he stormed out of the office.

Monteith returned, holding two cups of coffee. 'Who won?'

CHAPTER NINETEEN

Woody Anderson hadn't left Luke's bedside in the ICU since the previous day. The top of Luke's head was dressed, protecting the operational insertions where the surgeons had stemmed the bleeding and released the pressure on the brain. Now Luke was lying in a hospital bed with many wires attached: IV drips to keep him hydrated and for pain relief, and for monitoring his heart and blood pressure.

Doctors and nurses had regularly checked on Luke. A surgeon had come in late the previous evening and put Woody's mind at ease, confirming the operation had gone well. It was now just a case of waiting for the swelling to go down. Once that happened, they would slowly bring Luke out of his induced coma.

Andrew had remained with him for the first few hours before going to Freddie, who was on the orthopaedic ward. His leg looked like it had been put back together by an engineering company. Metal rods through the leg connected to two stainless steel rings with nuts, bolts, and wire. Andrew couldn't work out if they were trying to turn his brother into the bionic man or the terminator.

The nurses finally persuaded Woody to get something to eat, as they were washing Luke and changing his bed. He went to the toilet and splashed water on his face before meeting Andrew in the cafeteria.

From there, they went to check on Freddie.

'How's Luke?' Freddie asked as soon as they came through the door.

'Alive,' was all Woody said.

'When are we going to get the Claytons back?' Freddie demanded, his face taut with anger.

'I don't see how we can,' Andrew answered. 'You and Luke are in here, and me and Dad are on bail. We can't go near them.'

'Bail is nothing,' Woody said dismissively. 'The only reason we are out is because of Luke. We would still be answering their stupid questions if not.'

'But we can't go near them.'

'Bollocks,' his father exclaimed. 'This needs to end now. Luke is in a coma and Freddie here is looking like a Meccano set. They need to pay for doing this. Big time. Ring around and find where they are now. Fuck bail. The Claytons are dead meat.'

He got up and signalled for Andrew to leave. Walking through the lively atrium of the hospital, full with visitors and patients, Woody smiled inwardly. If only they knew what he was up to... The Clayton brothers deserved everything that would come at them, he thought grimly. How dare the jumped-up punks challenge them? They were nobody. Their name didn't even deserve to be said in the same breath as his family. And what was all this pally pally with the two detectives? He couldn't understand it. Two other people for them to cower behind and run to when they needed to.

Andrew and Woody came out into the bright afternoon sunlight as Speedy pulled up in a car he had just stolen. Andrew jumped in the front, Woody in the back.

'You have everything?' Woody wheezed. Hospitals were full of infections, and he was coming down with one.

'Yes, boss,' Speedy replied, looking at him through the rear-view mirror.

'Good, let's get this over and done with.'

Monteith ran down the stairs and caught up with Watson outside the interview room accommodating the Clayton brothers.

'Hey, why the rush? I was getting coffee,' Monteith said, gasping for breath.

'I need to get this over and done with,' Watson snapped, one hand on the doorknob, the other holding the file Sandall had given him.

'What? The interview? What's in the file?' He held out his hand.

Watson looked at the file before handing it over.

'Bloody hell!' Monteith exclaimed once he read it. 'This is a definite match?'

'Must be. I assumed we'd heard the last of him when he gave up.' Watson let go of the doorknob and leant against the wall, his anger subsiding.

'What are we going to do now? We've no way of finding him?'

'WE are doing nothing. *I* am going after this bastard,' Watson spat.

'Neither of you are doing anything.' The voice of DSI Wright echoed down the corridor as she strode towards them. 'Give me the file.' She held out her hand.

'But... ma'am,' Watson protested, taking the file from Monteith. 'I need to catch this bastard.'

'No buts. The file.'

Watson looked at the file, then at Wright as he begrudgingly handed it back.

'Paul showed me the file before you, and I made a few inquiries, so I know the back story. Uniform has been asked to keep an eye out for him. We will track him down.'

'We could hope he rings you again,' Monteith said.

'When was the last time he made contact?' Wright asked.

Watson thought. 'Not since Tuesday.'

'So, he could be due for another call?'

'Who knows what is going through that warped mind of his,' Watson sighed.

'Okay, here's what WE are going to do,' Wright stated firmly. 'You two are going to finish interviewing the Claytons and get as much information as you can.' She waved the file. 'We will deal with this later. Keith, make sure Terry does not leave the station or you will be in trouble.'

Monteith grinned. 'Can I handcuff him to the desk?'

'I don't care *how* you do it; just make sure it's done.' Wright turned on her heels and walked away.

Watson smirked. 'Handcuffs?'

Davy was agitated again, much to Watson's annoyance.

'Davy, sit down,' he ordered, to no avail.

Billy attempted to bring his brother back to the table, but Davy shook him off.

'The Andersons wanted to kill me. Why haven't you arrested them?' he exclaimed. His face was red with rage, hands balled into fists, looking like a bull ready to charge.

'When we have finished taking your statement, we will arrest the culprits. So the sooner you cooperate, the sooner they are arrested.'

Billy gave up persuading his brother to join them. 'Mr Watson, please, let's continue.' He turned to Davy. 'When you are ready, sit down. He moved Davy's chair towards the table.

Monteith kept an eye on Davy as Watson continued, 'Billy, can you tell us what led to the ambush the other morning?'

Billy leant back in his chair. 'Yes and no.'

'Explain.'

'Yes, I can tell you what led up to it, but no - I can't tell you what happened as we were not there.' He nodded at his brother as he explained about the meeting in the Royal Oak.

'You've mentioned that before, a meeting,' Watson stated. 'Now is the time for details. Who were there?'

'Sorry, Mr Watson, I'm not going to tell you that.'

Watson was annoyed. 'You want our protection, but you refuse to help us.'

'I cannot, Mr Watson. Remember the Kirk Douglas film? "I'm Spartacus. No, I'm Spartacus." The Andersons wanted us off the estate and our friends defended us. End of story.'

Speedy pushed the car through the built-up traffic towards their target.

Woody was fidgeting and getting worked up.

'Sorry boss, it's the roadworks,' Speedy apologised.

'Just make sure we get there before they leave.' His voice was threatening.

It was all the incentive Speedy needed. He shot down a side street and speeded up. Ten minutes later, they were parked at their target: police headquarters.

'They're still here, Dad,' Andrew said, pointing towards Davy's Vauxhall at the far end of the public car park.

'You know what to do.' Woody sat forward, staring through the gap in the front seats at the main doors. Speedy and Andrew got out and moved to the boot. Opening it, Speedy took out two baseball bats and Andrew a twelve-inch knife. Their movements stealthy, to avoid any suspicion.

Andrew, the knife tucked in his jacket, walked across to Davy's Vauxhall. After checking again for witnesses, he slashed both front tyres.

Watson and Monteith escorted Billy and Davy from the interview room into the reception. They paused just in front of the main doors.

'I suggest both of you keep a low profile,' Watson said. 'And don't think you're free. At the very least, you are complicit in this assault.'

'Try to not start anything,' Monteith added.

'What about finishing it?' Davy shouted, storming out.

It took a few moments for Watson, Monteith, and Billy to realise what was going on. Quickly, they rushed out the door after Davy.

On the stairs, they stopped in shock. Before them were Woody, Andrew, and Speedy with baseball bats and knives in hand.

Watson stepped forward. 'Mr Anderson, what are you playing at? Remember, you are on bail.'

'Fuck bail. Those bastards put two of my sons in the hospital. Luke could have brain damage or worse, die,' Woody snarled, pointing at Billy and Davy.

'The people of the estate sent you a message. Telling you they have had enough. Enough of your bullying and threats. Go away while you still can,' shouted Billy.

Woody strode towards the bottom steps. 'Bollocks. You set us up.'

Billy vehemently shook his head. 'You set yourselves up for a beating. Acting like the estate belonged to you when Dad died. Why the fuck could you not leave everything as it was? Instead, you wanted it all. Why do you think you were attacked? You got greedy and let your guard down. Became sloppy. We knew you would try to take us out. Hell, you even told us.' He paused, and said, calmer now, 'You didn't think all those families crossed over because they like you? They did it to get inside information, and you received them with open arms. *That's* how we knew you were coming for us.' Billy held his hands up. 'We are sorry that Luke and Freddie ended up in hospital, Luke especially.'

'No, no. You are lying,' Woody exclaimed. 'I don't believe you. You set it up, like the fire in my garage.'

'We didn't do that, did we, Speedy?' Davy snarled. 'Sure, we thought about doing something, even took a couple of reckies. But on the night we planned the fire, Speedy beat us to it.'

'What?' Woody exploded. He turned to Speedy.

'I didn't... They're lying. I wouldn't...' Speedy stuttered.

'Woody, I *saw* him,' Davy added. 'When the fire started, he came out and jumped the fence into the sports field. Later he came back when the emergency services were there, acting as if he had only just arrived.'

Speedy's face turned ashen. He was shaking uncontrollably, rubbing the palms of his hands on his clothes. 'It was an accident. I swear. I was cleaning up. I couldn't stop it, it went rapidly. I was afraid to tell you...' he stuttered, his voice barely audible.

'I know, I know, I believe you,' Woody said, putting his hand on Speedy's shoulder. With the other, he sank his knife deep into Speedy's abdomen. Twice, three times. Speedy slumped to the ground, holding his stomach with both hands, blood pouring out.

Davy saw his chance and launched himself straight at Woody.

Andrew swung his baseball bat and hit Davy full on the right arm. It didn't stop Davy, who charged Woody, sending them both crashing into the front of a Volvo. Andrew lifted his bat again, but before he could swing it at Davy, Monteith wrestled him to the ground. The bat was knocked free and rolled underneath another car.

Watson and Billy rushed towards Davy and Woody. Woody rolled over, picked up the knife, and aimed it at Davy. He caught the top of Davy's leg, slicing through jeans and flesh. Davy growled in pain as another swipe cut through his arm. Enraged, he landed a punch on Woody's face with his good arm.

Before either could inflict any further suffering on the other, they were jumped on and disarmed by five uniformed officers who held and cuffed them both. Andrew had been overpowered by Monteith, who put handcuffs on him.

Watson read a cursing Woody and subdued Andrew their rights. 'Woody Anderson, Andrew Anderson, you are both under arrest for assault, GBH, murder, attempted murder - and that's just for starters. Get them out of here.'

Search warrants for the Andersons and Claytons were immediately applied for; Matthews made certain they were top priority.

Woody and Andrew were languishing in the cells downstairs, screaming for their solicitor. Davy had been taken to A&E by ambulance to have the deep knife wounds treated. Billy and PC Kendall escorted him.

The car park and the front of the headquarters were screened off, and the road closed with crime scene tape so Mac and the SOCO team could do their work. The press had arrived en masse, but kept at a distance.

As soon as the warrants were issued, the police swarmed the Thelwell Estate, hitting everything the Andersons and the Claytons controlled. Houses, garages, they left nothing out. Anyone with an association with either family was struck. For the second time in less than twenty-four hours, the cells were full of Thelwell residents.

Most would be released on bail pending further inquiries. But a few on the Claytons' side were arrested and charged over the riot and attack on the Anderson family. Arrests on the Anderson team included those involved in stealing and re-assembling stolen cars were arrested. Drugs, baseball bats, and a vast array of stolen items were recovered from both sides.

Watson and Monteith led the sweep on Woody Anderson's home.

'And they say crime doesn't pay,' Monteith joked as they walked around the lavishly furnished detached house.

'Nowhere near the opulence of Jimmy Russell's pad, but even minor criminals have some taste nowadays,' Watson admitted.

'Detectives, up here,' a SOCO called from the landing. They both took the stairs two at a time. In the master bedroom, laid out on the bed, were three leather-bound drug kits containing vials and needles. 'We discovered them at the back of the wardrobe.'

'Personal use?' Monteith said.

'No way, not a chance,' Watson dismissed it. 'Why three and why put them at the back of a wardrobe if they were for personal use? He has hidden these for a reason.' He directed the SOCO to bag and tag them.

'You think Woody used one of them on Davy?'

'I guess we'll find out later.'

They watched out of the bedroom window at the examination below. Teams of SOCO and uniformed police were going through bins and the adjoining garage. Sandall appeared from what looked like a summerhouse and spotted them. He signalled for them to join him.

'What have you got, Paul?' Watson asked, crossing the well-kept lawn.

Paul passed him an evidence bag.

'Logbooks and registration papers. Looks like they were made here. Everything neatly filed and documented. Printers and computers all set up. SOCO is taking photos of everything here before bagging it.'

Watson looked at the evidence bag. 'Once we have all this back at headquarters, we need to identify who the Andersons sold these cars to. They are death traps waiting to happen. If one of these is involved in an accident, I don't hold out much hope for whoever is inside them.'

'Can we get this out of the way first?' Monteith asked. 'I'm already knackered, and Matthews wants us down there at 4.30 a.m tomorrow.'

Watson agreed. 'Paul, can I leave you to liaise with SOCO until they have finished?'

Walking back to the car, Watson looked at his watch, just after half past seven. 'I thought you stayed up all night when working at the casino.'

'I did, but I was getting in at 4.30 a.m. not starting then. I need my beauty sleep.'

Watson grinned. 'Believe me, no amount of sleep will make you beautiful.'

Monteith threw a hurtful expression. 'And I thought you loved me.'

'Get in the car, Sleeping Beauty.'

CHAPTER TWENTY

Friday

RAIN DRIFTED DOWN IN a fine mist. The truck had arrived fifteen minutes earlier, parking up in front of the Wild West Deliveries unit. Whiteman and Greatbatch were busy driving forklifts, unloading pallets from the trailer, and taking them into the unit. A red metal barred container filled with parcels of all sizes was inside the unit's roll-topped door. Drivers and other employees were sorting the parcels out, adding them to the ever-growing piles behind their delivery vans.

The last item to come off the trailer was a huge sealed metal unit, with padlocks and ziplocks over the lid for security. If the zip lock arrived broken, someone had tampered with it between leaving the depot and arriving at its destination. And the driver would have a lot of explaining to do. Its contents were valuable and only a few individuals knew what it contained.

At 5.30 a.m., James McGill turned his Mercedes through the gates of the industrial estate. The car's headlights cut through the gloom of the rain. Parking in his reserved spot, McGill took his coat off the backseat and put it on. His briefcase and newspaper followed. Locking the car, he entered the unit, noting everything before him. Standing close to his office was the sealed unit. McGill smiled and patted it before putting his coat, newspaper, and briefcase in his office. Travis Whiteman was examining the unit when McGill came back out, handing his boss the inventory list.

McGill's smile became broader. 'When they said it would be significant, they weren't joking.' He ran his finger down the list, taking in the magnitude of the deliveries. Deliveries that would set them up for life. Get them wrong, and all hell would break loose.

'Bloody hell, I've not seen this many drugs in one place before,' Whiteman exclaimed.

McGill laughed. 'You'll be seeing a lot more after we deliver this. I see good things happening to all of us. We're going places.'

'Miami for me,' Whiteman grinned.

'More like Skegness or Blackpool. Come on, time is money. Let's get it on the vans and out of here.'

The drug unit was standing by for the go-ahead to launch the raid. Even though Watson, Monteith, and Lorimer had been ordered to attend, they now felt the rising excitement and were eager to take part.

Underwood and Costa went over the orders for the raid. Word had come through from London that this was the biggest haul the gang had ever tried.

The radio crackled. It was the spotter in the overlooking office block. 'Unit number one opened. Packages being given to drivers for delivery. Over.'

Costa picked up his radio. 'Thanks, Matt. Let us know when the first van is ready to go. Over.'

'They had better be quick. I'm freezing my nuts off up here.'

'Everyone, gather round, please,' said Costa. 'Right. London had declared that raids have already taken place at the main hub in London, and the county depot in Cambridge. We have struck the jackpot on this. All the outlining depots, including this one, are a go. When Matt says they're rolling, two cars from the local force will block the estate, stopping them from fleeing. When that happens, we make a move. Take the drivers out first. They must not leave this estate,' he emphasised. 'Me, Underwood, and the three detectives from the local force,' Costa waved a hand in Watson, Monteith, and Lorimer's direction, 'will apprehend McGill and Whiteman and secure the drugs that have not been put in vans.'

Monteith whispered to Watson, 'He can't even introduce us, the prick.'

The radio crackled again. 'Vans are on the move. Repeat: on the move.'

'GO, GO, GO,' Costa shouted, throwing open the unit's main door.

Watson grabbed his radio. 'KENDALL, BLOCK THE GATES NOW.'

Within seconds, Kendall moved into position, putting his squad car square in the estate's entrance with another stopping next to him. Just in time, as the first van came to a shuddering halt in front of them. Before the driver had a chance to reverse, armed officers surrounded the van.

Shaun Greatbatch nudged his van out of the unit. Spotting the police at the gates, he jumped out. 'BOSS, BOSS. THE PO-LICE...' was all he got out before being wrestled to the ground.

Whiteman came out of the office. 'What was that, Shaun?'

'POLICE, POLICE. STOP WHERE YOU ARE!' Costa bellowed as he led the drug agency's cavalry charge into the unit.

'FUCK,' Whiteman exclaimed as he was wrestled to the ground and handcuffed. 'BOSS! THE POLICE!'

McGill scrambled to his feet, launching his desk chair towards the wall behind him. 'SHIT.' He rushed to seize the inventory paperwork off the top of the metal cabinet. Before he could reach it, Costa blocked his way. 'We'll take that.' He picked the paperwork off the floor.

McGill tried to make a run for it.

'Going somewhere?' Watson stood in front of him in the door, Monteith close behind.

'FUCK OFF,' McGill shouted, throwing punches at Watson. Watson dodged the first couple and countered with one of his own, knocking McGill back. Quickly, they had McGill face down on the desk with the cuffs on.

'I'm going to get you for assault, you bastard. Wait till I see your boss, Matthews. You'll be back on the beat in no time,' McGill raged.

Monteith hauled him up. 'You were resisting arrest. Oh, by the way... James McGill, you are under arrest for the murders of Evan Ferguson and Ryan Craven.'

He dragged McGill outside to a waiting police van. Whiteman and Greatbatch, also in handcuffs, were placed in the rear of separate police vans and taken back to headquarters for processing.

'Where are you taking McGill?' Costa exclaimed.

'Mr McGill here, Travis Whiteman, and Shaun Greatbatch are all under arrest for murder,' Monteith said.

'No, no.' Costa shook his head. 'No way. They are all under arrest for drug and narcotics distribution and will be taken back to London for questioning.'

Watson stepped in. 'DI Monteith, will you look after our prisoner? It seems DCI Costa has something he wishes to debate with me, DCI to DCI.'

Monteith walked off.

'What are you playing at? McGill and the rest are ours,' snapped Costa.

'Are you certain?' Watson replied in a calm voice. 'Thank you for helping with the arrest. You got what you came for. To take down a drug ring and you've done that. James McGill and his companions are wanted here for murder.'

'You can't do that. Your boss gave us the go-ahead and said you will cooperate. McGill is ours.'

'It's marvellous to see you two getting on so well,' Chief Superintendent Matthews declared, showing up out of the dawn darkness and drizzle with DSI Wright. 'Did everything go as planned, DCI Watson?'

Watson smiled. 'Yes sir, thank you. All drugs were recovered, and we have arrested those culpable. DCI Costa and I were just discussing our favourite person - James McGill.'

'Will you inform your DCI that we are taking McGill back to London?' Costa asked Matthews with an air of superiority to his voice.

'No, DCI Costa, I will not,' Matthews retorted. 'James McGill, Travis Whiteman, and Shaun Greatbatch are wanted here for two brutal crimes. As such, they will remain here.'

Costa looked shocked. 'But sir, we had a deal.'

'We did, that's right. But I spoke to your boss, DSI Andrews, and after I pointed out why we wanted McGill, he agreed to it. Nice man, I could get on with him.'

Costa stood frozen, his eyes switching from Matthews to Wright to Watson. He opened his mouth, but nothing came out.

'You can talk to him yourself. Here, use my phone.' Matthews took his phone out of his raincoat's pocket. 'It's on speed dial. Do you want me to?'

'No sir,' Costa mumbled, clearly taken aback. He shuffled off.

'Oh, and DCI Costa? He said make certain all the drugs recovered ARE brought back.'

Monteith and Watson looked at the receding figure of Costa. 'You'd almost feel sorry for him,' Monteith grinned.

'When did you get here?' Watson asked as they walked towards Wild West Deliveries Unit.

Wright replied, 'About ten minutes ago. We've been observing from the car back there. Looks like you have everything covered.'

'Yes, apart from Costa. Good thing you turned up when you did. Who knows what I would have done.'

'You would have done the right thing, DCI Watson,' Wright replied with an ironic grin and a wink.

'Yes, ma'am.' Watson winked back.

A loud voice broke the conversation. 'GRANT, GRANT.' McGill shouted through the open back door of the police van.

Matthews strolled over to the van and squinted in. 'James, I didn't realise you were in there.'

'There's been some colossal mistake; surely we can work something out.'

'You're right, James. I made a mistake.' Matthews clasped his hands behind his back. 'In becoming golfing partners with you. Listening to you whining every weekend. And later when you started complaining about my officers, saying that you and your company were being victimised, that was the final straw.'

'Your detective there,' McGill pointed towards Watson. 'He assaulted me. I want him charged.'

'You probably deserved it,' Matthews said. 'Oh, one further thing, James. The golf club's committee members blackballed you last night and revoked your membership.'

One week later

The church car park was filling up as the Ravenswood CID gathered for the funeral of former DSI Kenneth Crompton.

Although the family had initially requested a family-only funeral, they had relented when Matthews had told Kenneth's widow, Edith, that he and other colleagues from the Ravenswood police wanted to carry the coffin.

They were all present: Matthews and Wright, Watson, Monteith, Lorimer, French, and Sandall. They made their way to the church entrance to wait for the cortege to arrive.

Watson glanced around the family and friends of their former boss. Some he knew, most he didn't. Two women were standing at a distance. Two women he knew. Tapping Monteith on the shoulder, he pointed them out.

'Well, well. I wondered if they would turn up,' commented Monteith.

Watson walked up to the two. 'Hello Angie,' he said.

Angie McDonald smiled. 'Hello, Detective Chief Inspector. I just had to see him off, I'll be out of the family's way but... he's been a friend.'

'I know,' said Watson. He turned to Elizabeth Freeman Preston. 'And hello to you. I know from what Kenneth told me you and he were close once.'

A pair of teary eyes set on him. 'Once, I thought... but then all the bad things happened. My brother in jail. Then, when free, murdered. And Kenneth back in my life. Ironic, isn't it?'

He nodded as he said his goodbye and went back to the church.

The cortege slowly moved up and reached the church doors.

After offering their respects to Edith and the rest of the family, Sandall escorted Wright and French into the church, leaving Matthews, Watson, Monteith, and Lorimer to carry the coffin in.

Elizabeth Preston and Angie McDonald followed at a distance, entering the church after everybody else, sitting right at the back.

The after-funeral gathering was held at the neighbouring church hall, sufficient for the thirty-odd attendees. Tales and anecdotes about Crompton and his police career were shared, apart from the last one. That remained unspoken.

A Month Later

The last month had been exceptionally busy.

James McGill, Travis Whiteman, and Shaun Greatbatch were all charged with the murders of Evan Ferguson and Ryan Craven, and refused bail. Also on the charge sheet was witness intimidation and arson, in connection to Geoffrey Henson and his farm. The drug charges were being held on file pending the conclusion of their court case.

Monteith and Sandall travelled to Lincoln to share the good news with Amanda Ferguson and her parents. Amanda told them she had put her house on the market and was moving to Lincoln. A fresh start was what she needed.

Watson and Monteith swung by Craven Autos to see Joey. As they parked up, Joey was locking up.

'What's with shutting up in the middle of the day?' Watson asked.

'It's for sale. With Ryan gone, along with McGill's money, we couldn't keep it running.'

'Are you going to buy it?'

'Looking at it. All the mechanics are clubbing together. We need to talk to the banks for a start-up loan, but they want a business plan.'

'Good luck with it. I may be the first client,' Monteith said.

Woody Anderson was charged with the murder of Steven 'Speedy' Rivers and the attempted murder of Davy Clayton. Andrew and Freddie were charged with GBH and aiding and abetting in the attempted murder of Davy Clayton. The charges against the whole family included the chop shop garages, handling stolen goods, and drug possession. The owners of twenty cars that had passed through their garages were tracked down, and the cars impounded. Some were considering legal action against the Andersons.

Luke Anderson died from his head injuries without coming out of his coma. The teenager who'd thrown the brick at Luke was caught and charged with his manslaughter. The man who attacked Freddie and broke his leg was also found and charged with GBH with intent.

The Claytons didn't get off scot-free. They were also charged with selling stolen property and drug possession. Lack of evidence prevented the police from charging them for the assault on the Andersons.

CHAPTER TWENTY ONE

THE WATSON AND MONTEITH families finally had a free weekend to celebrate Katie Monteith's unexpected pregnancy. Both had packed their children off to the in-laws for the weekend.

'I would like to propose a toast,' Watson said as he rose from the dining room table. 'Here's to the strongest and best friends anybody could have. Congratulations on the awaited new arrival to the Monteith household. To Keith and Katie.'

'Sit down, you daft bugger.' Monteith grinned.

'Have you thought of names yet?' Sally asked, putting her glass back down.

'This one wants to give the baby a Spanish name.' Katie rolled her eyes at Keith.

'Entirely appropriate seeing as it happened on holiday in Spain. I thought of either Miguel or Sierra.'

'Good thing you didn't travel to Russia. Igor or Olga. Oh no!' Watson exclaimed, his face in mock-disgust.

They all burst out laughing.

'Time for more refreshments,' Watson said, emptying the last drops of wine into Sally's glass, with an idiotic grin pasted on his face.

'Hey, don't get any ideas, Terry Watson. Three kids are enough for me.' Sally wagged a finger as he got up.

'Who me? Never crossed my mind,' Watson replied, feigning innocence before heading into the kitchen. Opening the fridge, he thought back to not so long ago when their friends' marriage had been close to ending because of Keith's gambling and the debts he owed the Russell brothers. Then finding out he was related to them. He shook his head. A miracle really, that now, barely six months later, they were cheerfully celebrating a new arrival. We are lucky, he thought.

As Watson grabbed a bottle of white wine, a John Smith's for Monteith, and a J2O for Katie, the phone rang.

'I'll take it,' he called out through to the dining room.

'Hello, Terry Watson speaking.'

'Miss me?' said a frosty voice.

Watson's blood froze at the sound of the altered voice. Hairs on the back of his neck and arms stood up on end. The bastard was back. 'What the fuck do you want?' he shouted.

'Nothing. Just calling to see how you are. I stopped because you were so hectic with the Thelwell Estate and James McGill. I require your full attention.'

Monteith appeared at the kitchen door and mouthed, 'Is it him?'

Watson nodded. 'You have my complete attention now, former Detective Constable Richard Walker.'

He heard a sharp intake of breath. Then the voice of Walker now, without alteration. 'Aha. You're not a Detective Chief Inspector for nothing, are you? What was it?'

Watson's hatred surged. 'You left fingerprints on the photographs, you sick bastard. If you come close to my family again, I'll...'

'You'll WHAT? Kill me? Terry, we know that won't happen. You're one of the good guys. Lets everyone else get their hands dirty.' The voice was bitter.

Monteith closed the door and stood close to Watson, struggling to listen in.

'What the hell do you mean?'

'Come now, you've not forgotten. All the time we worked together, and you've not worked it out yet?'

'Stop talking in riddles, Walker.' Watson was getting pissed off.

Sally stuck her head around the door, a bemused expression on her face.

Monteith put a finger to his lips and steered her out. 'Nothing to worry about, just work stuff.' He closed the door behind her.

As he did they, heard the front doorbell.

'I'll get it,' Sally shouted.

'Shame you haven't worked it out. Listen, I have to run now,' Walker declared. 'No rest for the wicked. Oh, tell your wife she looks stunning.' With that, Walker was gone.

Watson stared at the phone. 'Your wife looks stunning,' he mouthed, staring at Monteith. 'SHIT... SALLY NOOOO.' Watson's legs felt like they were in treacle and the world was moving in slow motion as he launched himself at the kitchen door.

He flung it wide as Sally opened the front door. The noise of gunshots resounded through the blackness outside. Watson rushed into the hallway and dropped to his knees. Before him was Sally, slumped on the front doorstep, covered in blood.

'SSSAAAAALLLLLYYYYY!!'

THE END

TONY MILLINGTON

Tony Millington is the author of the *Ravenswood Crime Series*, comprising five books, of which three have been published currently. Set in the fictional city of Ravenswood, DCI Watson and his sidekick, DI Monteith, are the lead detectives of the city's police force.

Prior to writing, Tony spent many years as a civil servant in the MOD, working on local RAF bases. Also, he worked for the local council in Adult and Children's Social Care. He originates from Cheshire, and moved down to Rutland when he was thirteen. He now lives in Cambridgeshire and has been happily married for over twenty-six years; the couple has a son.

Tony volunteers as a facilitator in Peterborough for AMC (Andy's Man Club) charity, a men's suicide prevention charity.

When not writing and walking his Romanian rescue dog, Mira, or catering to the demands of his cat Lucky, you can find Tony rocking out to heavy metal.

Tony Millington on social media:
Facebook: TonyMillingtonAuthor
Twitter: @TonyMillington9

CITY STONE PUBLISHING

*Indie publisher with a passion for the written word
and a heart that beats for authors everywhere*

We are an imaginative and enthusiastic indie publisher.

Our ambition is twofold:

To develop outstanding books and work alongside our authors.

To be a beacon of advice and a provider of services for indie authors.

We are not just about the books; we build relationships with our authors. Because we both write, we know what (indie) authors want. That is how we work: in cooperation and partnership with our authors.

From dark and gritty crime thrillers, adventurous fantasy, entertaining women's fiction, and intriguing contemporary novels to interesting and insightful non-fiction and visionary poetry, we publish it all.

Visit our website: citystonepublishing.com

CSP

ANDY'S MAN CLUB

ANDYSMANCLUB are a men's suicide prevention charity, offering free-to-attend peer-to-peer support groups across the United Kingdom and online.

Their goal is to end the stigma surrounding men's mental health and help men through the power of conversation.

ANDYSMANCLUB want to eliminate the stigma surrounding mental health and create a judgment-free, confidential space where men can be open about the storms in their lives.

They aim to achieve this through weekly, free-to-attend peer-to-peer support groups for men aged over 18.

#ITSOKAYTOTALK
www.andysmanclub.co.uk

TONY MILLINGTON

ACKNOWLEDGEMEN

I would like to thank Caroline and Jon at City Stone Publishing for all their hard work in publishing this book. I know readers have been waiting for a long time for *Battle Lines* to hit the shelves. It's hung around in the files on my computer for the last four years. Now thanks to Caroline's hard work and due diligence it has finally arrived.

Huge thanks go out to BETA readers Maureen Davies and Beryl Fielder.

I would like to thank former senior detective Graham Bartlett for his help and the advice he has given regarding the correct ranks of the police force, and how to make my books authentic.

To Kerrie Watson and Kerry Monteith. The original Watson and Monteith double act. Ladies, it was a pleasure working with you.

To my friends at Andy's Man Club Peterborough, who help me see the end of the tunnel when I am struggling with writing and remind me of how far I have come in a short time.

To Sam Brownley and Caroline Maston, the ladies behind the UK Crime Book Club on Facebook. Aimed at discussing and promoting UK-based crime fiction authors. Thank you for all your hard work.

To fellow authors, Ross Greenwood, Donna Morfett, Liz Mistry, Tony Forder, Malcolm Hollingdrake, Wes Markin, J.C. Macek III, Catherine Yaffe, Alistair Birch, Chris Blackwater, Eoghan Egan, Sarah Moorhead, Louise Mullins for the support you have given me through out the past years. If I have left anyone else out... Sorry.

And last but no means least, to you my readers. Thank you for purchasing *Battle Lines*. I hope you have enjoyed it. Please leave a review on Amazon and Goodreads, or any other review sites.